Gerry Anderson's

<u>THE DAY AFTER TOMORROW</u>
INTO INFINITY

The crew of the Altares (*L-R*): Martin Lev *as David Bowen,* Joanna Dunham *as Anna Bowen,* Brian Blessed *as Tom Bowen,* Katharine Levy *as Jane Masters, and* Nick Tate *as Captain Harry Masters.*

Gerry Anderson's

THE DAY AFTER TOMORROW
INTO INFINITY

A Novel by
Gregory L. Norris
Based on the Teleplay by
Johnny Byrne

ANDERSON
ENTERTAINMENT

Gerry Anderson's
THE DAY AFTER TOMORROW
INTO INFINITY

First published in Great Britain by Anderson Entertainment Ltd., 2017
Second edition 2019

THE DAY AFTER TOMORROW/INTO INFINITY novel and
'Afterword' copyright © 2017 by Gregory L. Norris
THE DAY AFTER TOMORROW/INTO INFINITY copyright © 1975 and
2017 by Anderson Entertainment Ltd.
Frontispiece photo © 1975 and 2019 by Anderson Entertainment Ltd.

The moral rights of the author have been asserted.

Freely adapted from THE DAY AFTER TOMORROW/INTO INFINITY
teleplay written by Johnny Byrne.

All characters in this publication are fictitious and any resemblance to real
persons, living or dead, is purely coincidental.

All rights reserved.
No part of this publication may be reproduced, stored in a retrieval
system, or transmitted, in any form or by any means, without the prior
permission in writing of the publisher, nor be otherwise circulated in any
form of binding or cover other than that in which it is published and
without a similar condition including this condition being imposed on the
subsequent purchaser.

ISBN **978-1091390393**

Editor: Robert E. Wood
Cover Design: Martin Jones / martipants.co.uk

ANDERSON
ENTERTAINMENT

Anderson Entertainment Ltd.
Hornbeam House, Bidwell Road
Norwich, NR13 6PT

www.anderson-entertainment.co.uk

For Johnny Byrne, Gerry Anderson,
Joanna Dunham, and poet Tina Marie Perry,
fellow travelers and explorers of the great,
unknown universe.

Chapter One

On their charge up from the launch platform at Spaceport Alpha, Jane Masters attempted to recite a prayer in silence. When that failed, she thought of a favorite poem, but the words fell apart in her thoughts. The Space Authority passenger shuttle taking her and most of the crew up to Space Station Delta fought against gravity and the Earth as it boosted higher. Surely, they were past the troposphere by now, cutting stratosphere and headed toward the void. Somewhere up there, Delta awaited. And docked to an arm jutting forth from an outer section of the station was their ultimate destination: the light ship *Altares*.

Jane closed her eyes. The prayer formed, though not in her voice, but General Bishop's.

...protect us. To Space Station Delta – the jumping off point for Humanity's first momentous

journey to the stars!

The girl realized that the general's words were part of an early mission briefing, mostly meant for cameras and reporters. It had been delivered shortly after she and her father had been selected for the *Altares* team.

The light ship Altares, *the first of her kind to harness the limitless power of the photon — particles of light, which can boost her to velocities approaching the speed of light.*

General Bishop was good at making speeches that stoked your enthusiasm. Jane's excitement over the mission had matched if not exceeded even that of her father's, Harry Masters, *Altares'* captain.

The passenger shuttle shook. Jane's heart galloped. General Bishop's monologue continued in her memory for several seconds longer, talking about Einstein's Theory of Relativity, effects that could shrink the very fabric of space and distort time — that's what the five crew members would soon find themselves up against.

For the first stage of the mission, you will journey to Alpha Centauri, Bishop said. *The nearest star to our solar system. A mere twenty-four million, million miles from Earth.*

That measure of distance robbed Jane's lungs of air. Breathing ceased being involuntary or easy. Their loft at Spaceport Beta, her friends at school, the Earth itself...they were all part of a yesterday, now effectively over.

The shuttle ceased quaking and traveled ahead smoothly. They were out of the atmosphere and free of the Earth's gravity. A lightness came over Jane. Breathing resumed being easy again. The shuttle captain's voice droned from the intercom, said something about chasing the space station's orbit, ETA to Delta, and hoping for a decent ride the rest of the way.

Jane lifted the shade. The space window beside her seat looked out on a wash of dark sky and what had to be a thousand stars. Planet Earth was at their backs. Ahead, the enormous hulk of Space Station Delta was already visible. It grew with the seconds, an inelegant mass of interconnected bulky geometric shapes—blocky squares and half-circle domes, floating high above the globe.

From their approach angle, Jane caught sight of the light ship. *Altares* hung suspended above the space station, docked to the outer section opposite the supply and construction routes working to assemble the new Space Station Epsilon. Sleek and beautiful even from the distance, Jane caught herself smiling in reflection.

Earth was yesterday, *Altares* their tomorrow.

She settled back in her seat and watched the space station grow before them as the shuttle made its final approach.

The passenger shuttle glided into position and mated with the airlock, the connection textbook perfect. Jane unbuckled her safety harness and followed the man seated directly in front of her toward the exit.

Captain Harry Masters, a tall, athletic man with a neat haircut, cast a look over his shoulder and winked. Jane saw that her dad was smiling, too.

Four of the light ship's five crewmembers ambled along the vast concourse leading into Delta. Transparent sections on either side of the floor bridge showed Earth in the distance, and a good many of those thousand stars visible from their position in the galaxy. Around them rose walls and parts of the station's giant, complex machinery. Jane felt dwarfed on that long walk toward their destination. The echo of their footsteps, a small sound in a big space, added to the sensation.

Two of the Bowen family walked behind them—Tom Bowen, *Altares'* navigator, and his son, David. David, a boy with dark hair and an expression that was all business, followed at the large man's side. Like Jane, David was promised better training aboard the light ship than at any of the Space Authority's other programs.

No one spoke, she noted. Perhaps in such instances words, whether in prayer or uttered as poetry, weren't necessary, she mused. Jane imagined that her father and the Bowens had gone silent for the same reasons as she—the moment, the majesty and mission. *Altares,* docked high overhead, waited.

Einstein's time-dilation effect could create immense problems for the crew, Jane remembered from Bishop's speech for the reporters at Spaceport Alpha. *Upon return, they could find that thirty years may have elapsed, while they could only have been away for a fraction of the time.*

Additional sets of footsteps joined the crew's four, these moving faster to catch up. With them came the excited barking of a dog. It turned out that they weren't so far into tomorrow as Jane's imagination led her to believe.

The extra footsteps belonged to Anna Bowen, the fifth member of *Altares'* crew, and to Controller Jim Forbes, the man in charge of overseeing Delta. The small dog bounded over to her. Jane scooped her up in her arms at the doors of the *Altares* liftoff ramps.

She held the dog close against her, recording the moment in her thoughts for the future. To avoid the frightening dilemma of having adult crewmembers return home to find their children had grown older than they were, the Space Authority had deemed it necessary to send families intact on the mission. Even so, there was no room on the light ship for a dog.

Winter's tags jingled. Jane unclipped the one in the shape of a snowflake and pocketed it.

"Goodbye, Winnie," she said, her voice hitching with a sob. "Be good."

Forbes, an athletic older man clad in his

austere Space Station Delta uniform — white with black collar and matching stripes down both arms — leaned forward and picked up the dog.

"You'll take good care of her, won't you, sir?" Jane asked.

Forbes offered an understanding smile. "Of course I will, Jane."

The earlier rush of excitement she'd experienced at docking up with Delta was gone, smothered by a mix of guilt and loss. Unable to face Winnie, she plodded past the open elevator doors, joining the other crewmembers. Before the doors closed, Winnie struggled in the Controller's arms and cried out. The plaintive yelp, Jane thought, would always haunt her, no matter how far and long from Earth *Altares* traveled.

The lift doors closed. The elevator began to ascend through Space Station Delta, up toward the light ship.

There was so much else she remembered on the wait between the station and reaching *Altares*. Winnie, yes — they'd adopted Winter Masters on a cold late December day, right around Christmas, before applying for, being assigned, and training for the deep space exploration mission. Following her mother's death earlier that same autumn, Jane was sure she'd die from the sadness, but Winnie had helped her survive the loss. There were friends, yes, but most of them were before training at

Spaceport Beta. She liked David Bowen, she supposed, though they were hardly what she considered friends.

Everything they owned had been packed up and sent into storage at Beta, including her mother's belongings. Among those relics were the watercolors that Sylvia Masters had created — garden studies mostly, from a lost era before Beta, before Delta, before *Altares*. The flower garden at the house on Rankine Lane, past the flagstone patio. Jane remembered the beach roses, the purple pinwheel clematis, the white daisies with sunny-yellow centers, mostly through her mother's artwork, relics from the world that had been. There wasn't room aboard the light ship for dogs and the same held true for framed paintings.

It was possible that she'd never see those watercolors or anything else entombed in Unit 311 again. Jane's melancholy deepened.

A hand rested on her shoulder. Her father's gesture of comfort, done in actions without words, liberated her from her thoughts and brought Jane back to the moment — the elevator, whisking ever higher along its track outside the space station's superstructure and toward the metal dais upon which *Altares* perched, poised to make her historic launch. She was certain he meant to reassure her over Winnie, who'd been mostly her dog. Maybe he sensed she was mourning Sylvia Masters again, the other member of their small family not going to *Altares*.

By the time the elevator slowed to a stop and the lift doors opened, she'd swallowed down her sadness and was again composed. *Altares* welcomed them into its sturdy mass. The light ship's nose was aimed at deep space, and the infinity of star systems to be explored far beyond the Earth's.

Chapter Two

David Bowen exited the elevator first. They were no longer within Delta, but now standing directly outside the light ship. *Altares* waited beyond a corridor of panels lit in bright sun-yellow. The boy approached the inner airlock, a seamless round disk set into the wall. He keyed in his security code and the perfect circle shattered into four equal triangle wedges. The sections drew apart, bidding the crew entrance.

Jane hurried past him into the orderly, clean landscape of *Altares*, which would be their only home for the foreseeable future.

The holdall case hanging from David's fingers renounced the weight it had taken on during the distance from shuttle through concourse. There wasn't much inside the holdall, just a few personal things like photographs stored on a tablet, two decks of playing cards — one still in its unopened box, and several beloved books in print. The tablet also contained an entire library's worth of reading material; *Altares* data systems held even more, a trove of truths and fictions that couldn't possibly be read and experienced over the course of a single lifetime. Since the Space Authority logged and approved everything that would travel with them to the light ship, he'd opted to leave behind the raggedy stuffed bear missing an ear and one button eye.

To his mother Anna's chagrin, he'd tossed the refugee from his childhood into the bins of donations that would go to the less fortunate. In cooperation with the Earth Authority, the Space Authority had done an excellent job in alleviating global disease, poverty, and hunger. There remained plenty of distance to go, David supposed, even as the development of star-drive engines running on clean photon-generated power readied to put Earth at their backs and multitudes of unexplored star systems in front of them.

He hadn't packed clothes, no. Lockers in the Crew's Quarters contained numerous changes of the beige uniform shirts and chocolate and umber slacks — powder blue for the Masters family — and even several pairs of regulation boots and the comfortable jackets bearing the *Altares* Mission name and the Space Authority's insignia that completed the ensemble, if needed.

David cast a glance to his right—aft, where the deep space juggernaut's water storage tanks were visible and, farther along, those enormous pods containing the chemical rocket fuel for maneuvering and sub-light travel. At the farthest extreme of the neat succession of compartments and design was the sealed hatch leading to the Particle Acceleration Chamber. Nearer, the assembly of the Martin-B Photon Drive Unit was housed.

Energy thrummed up through the floor, the treads of David's boots, into his blood, his bones, and deeper past what he could only think of as his soul as he turned left toward the Crew's Quarters, the Monitoring Area, Navigation, and the Flight Deck. He'd stood in *Altares* before, marveling at the light ship's design, its beauty. But now was different, the emotion more intense. They were close to launch. Long last, all of the scientific wonders around him would be put to the test.

David drew in a deep, cleansing breath and then released it. The air aboard the light ship was warmer than on Space Station Delta, he observed. Warm as the summer air at home. Correction, he thought—*Altares* was now their home.

He stowed his holdall. Behind him, Harry Masters, their captain and the last to come on board the ship, activated his security code on the airlock controls. The four triangular sections rejoined into a circle and bolted into place. Even as David took to the Navigation Area, aware that his father was moving to catch up, the boy heard the hatch seal, a sharp, brief mechanical note that signaled they would soon depart the station, the Earth, and all that was familiar.

Sealed in, David thought.

His mind attempted to wander back to the centrifuge chamber at the spaceport's training facility, and the micro-gravity vault located among the Authority's laboratories on Delta. His lungs constricted. David turned behind him, expecting to see his father. It was easier to breathe in the large man's shadow. Only Tom Bowen was no longer there. *Altares'* walls had closed in, trapping him.

No, blink!

David obeyed his inner voice's urging. The bulkhead walls drew back to their proper distance. His father stood just inside the Crew's Quarters hatch, near Harry Masters. The two men exchanged a smile without words, a silent acknowledgement that they were soon to depart, all systems operational. All was well.

Their message to one another delivered, the two men marched forward into the Navigation Area. Harry Masters continued on through to the Flight Deck located in the command module, where Jane was setting up shop. Their captain patted David's shoulder as he passed. That small gesture removed the last of David's unease. Their crew, he agreed, was in great hands. *Altares* — and the Bowen family — couldn't have asked for a better captain and pilot than Harry Masters.

The 3-D flight simulator on Alpha bore an illusion of being solid thanks to a variation of the same photon-based tech set to carry them across the great distance that separated Sol from Alpha Centauri. Through those long hours and days — and a pair of interplanetary shakedown cruises, Mercury in one direction, Neptune in the opposite — Harry Masters had come to know *Altares* better than any man, including her designer.

The flight deck and instrumentation were solid under his boots and fingertips. The Flight Deck boasted two chairs, located close together beneath a forward-facing direct vision space window and an overhead screen, angled at the perfect reach. Around him, the array of computers and guidance systems gleamed, new and barely touched.

"All set?" Jane asked.

Masters tipped a glance toward the copilot's seat. Jane avoided his eyes while taking her position. Winter, he sensed. He nodded. "Sure am. You?"

This brought them face-to-face. His daughter's sad expression brightened.

"Jane," he started.

She turned away and resumed flipping switches on the screen angled down at them. The picture altered from a live-feed view of *Altares* beamed from the station's external cameras to the countdown clock, which mattered more than anything already gone by in those earlier seconds. Jane was fine, he sensed, and completely focused on her job.

Masters tapped another button on the controls. A pull-down screen appeared beside the countdown, spelling out the next step. Jane thumbed the ship-wide intercom in response.

"Crew stand by for pre-flight checks," Jane said.

There was awesome strength in her statement. Energy built around him—how much of it was *Altares* and what owed to his own heart hammering madly in his chest blurred. For a moment, Masters realized he was indistinguishable from the light ship, that they were one and the same creature. Pins and needles rocketed over his flesh and then beneath it.

"Power?" he asked.

Jane was busy carrying out her share of responsibility in their pre-flight list, punching buttons that then displayed readings above their heads. Everything was in the green.

"Internal, check," she reported. "All systems at optimum."

Jane's voice carried over the ship-wide, behind them into the Navigation Area. That section of the light ship boasted a balance of the latest tech laid out beside trusted and noble old—the chart table was outfitted with a screen that matched the pilot's, but sharing space on walls between computer terminals were physical star charts, most housed in rolls, some displayed like artwork.

"Guidance systems?" Masters called.

Bowen took to the chart table, his chair beside David's. "Active."

"And link to main computer."

David expelled the breath bottled inside his lungs and punched the proper sequence of buttons to carry out the captain's order. "Link up!"

Another check accomplished, another connection to the mother planet at their backs severed. David shifted in his seat and waited for the numbers counting down on his screen to run out.

For a moment, Anna Bowen wasn't aboard *Altares*, sitting alone in the great ship's Monitoring Area. She had returned to Controller Forbes' office on Delta. The screen suspended from a ceiling arm, its volume on low, broadcast World Television Network coverage of the preparations for *Altares'* launch. She tipped a glance away from Forbes to the screen and saw WTN was recycling old news, according to the image of the light ship, still a skeletal framework surrounded by girders and spotlights. The image altered into a familiar grid showing faces—the five crewmembers assigned to *Altares*.

"You've left it a bit late to turn us into television personalities, haven't you, Jim?" she asked, punctuating the statement with a laugh that sounded desperate even to her own ears.

Forbes shifted in his chair, closer to the corner of desk where she leaned. Anna tracked his approach from the cut of her eye, aware of her quickening pulse.

"You've been locked away in training. The whole world, from Alpha to what there is of Epsilon in orbit, will be watching this launch—the interest is unbelievable," he said, and how she'd grown to love his voice, its authority and also its mischief, that element meant only for her. "You're heroes."

Anna grinned, though the gesture belonged more to nerves than pride. "Is that why they're watching? I thought they wanted to see how we're spending their money up here."

"As an astronaut, you'd make a good politician, Anna."

His fingers inched closer to hers, now gripping the edge of his desk. At the moment of contact, energy crackled across her skin, curiously icy.

"Stay, Anna," Forbes said.

The cold vanished, driven out by a rush of imaginary heat. "You know I can't. It's too—"

Late. One of the instruments on the desk interrupted the statement with a musical chirp.

Forbes drew back from her touch and answered.

"This is Delta Control. Earth Shuttle Four has arrived."

"Right," Forbes said.

Anna glanced up. She was soon aware that Forbes refused to meet her eyes.

"Jim?"

"When the rest of the crew is on Delta, you'll be on the air for the last interview before departure...and make it good!"

He stood and extended the same hand that had sought her touch toward the exit, all the goodbye he'd offer.

And then she was back on *Altares*, sitting alone in the Monitoring Area. Anna thought she might cry but didn't.

Chapter Three

A home of a kind could have been made on Delta with Forbes. David could have shared in the responsibilities of caring for the Controller's new companion, Winnie. That version of Anna Bowen, living in an alternate reality, wouldn't have stayed without her son. She'd become infamous, even more of a celebrity than Forbes had predicted — the wife who left her husband right as they were readying to launch into deep space. David Bowen in either scenario would not have left his father's side.

Anna's eyes drifted from the monitoring instruments to the bunks and surrounding walls, a porthole on one side of her domain, the transparent safety partitions between crew and the entrance to the Photon Drive Chamber on the other. This was her home now, not on Delta with Forbes.

Masters' voice over the intercom brought her again to the moment. "Atmosphere?"

Anna moved to the screen monitoring that facet of their life support systems. "Balanced and stable."

"Artificial gravity?" the captain asked.

She scanned the readout, displayed beside the other important figures. "Nine point four degrees. Earth relative."

"Human stress factor?"

Even as she faced the monitor displaying all five crewmembers' vital signs, Anna sensed her pulse rate betraying her. To her relief, their readings were slightly elevated, no doubt owing to equal parts excitement and anxiety. Anna smiled to herself and actually felt better.

"Stress factor normal," she said.

"Time to liftoff?"

Bowen answered the captain's latest question. "Computerized. Three hundred and twenty seconds."

Four minutes, Anna thought. She mourned the possibilities of that other life with Jim Forbes as they faded like a barely remembered dream. Four minutes and counting down.

"Countdown continues," her son said.

Masters cast a glance at the overhead screen. Soon, he thought. "Activate navigation controls."

Tom Bowen moved from his seat at the

chart table to the wall of instruments running at his right. The computer terminal over the navigation tech flared to life, reading 2459. Bowen removed the proper disks and plugged them into the navigation computer's waiting trays. The results were instantaneous — and breathtaking. Live-feed images of their course beamed onto the chart table's screen.

"Navigation codes activated," said David.

"And check radiation screens," said Masters, finally at the end of his pre-launch checklist. The last step between Delta and the void.

Anna left the monitoring instruments, crossed the Crew's Quarters, and approached the light propulsion engine complex, whose core was sealed behind a dense protective circular door. A sign warned in flashing red letters: PHOTON DRIVE. She pressed a switch. Amber light bathed the division between the door and dual transparencies.

"Heat screens operative," she reported.

Jane stowed her copilot's copy of the checklist. "Checks complete."

Masters thumbed the button on the radio that put them through to the space station. "How do we look, Delta?"

A man's voice from Delta Control answered. "Pretty good, *Altares*...all systems go. We're just running a final check on your telemetry system."

"Switch to visual," Masters said.

The image of space and stars beamed on their screens from the chart table changed to that of Controller Forbes, seated at his office desk on Delta, with Winnie in his lap.

"This is it, Harry," Forbes said. "For the last time, good luck and goodbye."

"Till we meet again," Masters said.

Forbes smiled, nodded. "Well...I may not be around when you youngsters return. Old age could have got me or something."

Arms behind her back, Anna shuffled into the Flight Deck. Bowen and David hovered in the arch between cockpit and Navigation, taking in the exchange.

"You, Jim, you're indestructible," she said.

The smile dropped from Forbes' face. "Don't be so sure. We armchair pilots have our problems, too."

Problems like me, she thought. But not for much longer.

Anna didn't respond to the dig, a secret shared only by two. There was no need to. In seconds, one of the bearers of that secret would be traveling at the front of a comet accelerating to speeds close to matching that of light. The Controller's problem was going away. He'd no doubt find a new interest to share his life with on Delta, whereas she'd take their secret with her, across unimaginable distances.

"Telemetry check positive," Delta Control chimed in. "Liftoff in sixty seconds."

"We'll maintain satellite linkup via Delta Beacon as long as possible so you can see how you look from the cameras in space," Forbes said. "Well, good luck until we meet again."

He saluted.

"Goodbye, Jim," Masters said.

Her son, husband, and their copilot offered similar farewells, Anna's voice lost in the small chorus. Even before Masters gave the order to strap in, she had turned away from the screen and was exiting the Flight Deck.

It's done, thought Anna. She'd made her choice.

Bowen and David assumed their seats behind the chart table and buckled their safety harnesses. She ran a hand through her son's hair, messing it out of its neatness, and cast a smile at her husband. The decision was the correct one, she knew.

Anna took to the Monitoring Area's medical couch and strapped in. Those last remaining seconds in the wake of official *au revoirs* with Delta Station, Jim Forbes, Earth, and everything that was tolled with the weight of hours.

"Thirty seconds," said the voice from Delta Control over the radio.

Anna closed her eyes. When they again opened, it was a whole new life.

And universe.

Altares faced the great unknown and

unexplored reaches of space beyond Earth's solar system. At minus twenty-five seconds, the last of the magnetic anchors securing the light ship to Delta Station's West Docking Port relaxed its grip. At twenty, steering rockets activated, boosting the metal giant up, up. Thus freed, *Altares* hovered.

Aboard, Bowen regarded his son with pride and flashed a rare smile. Anna cleared her thoughts. Pilot and copilot prepared for the countdown to run out.

"Pre-ignition," Masters ordered.

Jane thumbed the switch. The graceful giant, floating in place, rumbled as the colossal bell rockets fixed to her sub-light engines lit in readiness.

"Ten seconds," the voice from Delta Control reported. "Five…four…three…"

Masters closed his eyes and offered a brief and silent prayer to whatever deity was listening.

"Two…one…*zero*."

His eyes again shot open. "Ignition!"

"Ignition," Jane repeated.

Altares' chemical rockets fired. The light ship raced away from her perch above Delta like a missile and soon cleared the space station. She arrowed forward at a tremendous velocity, the opening charge sending the light ship thousands of miles in seconds. Less than a minute after launch, she was closer to Earth's moon than the primary planet. The satellite's cinder and lava face rose at starboard.

Speed achieved, the bell rockets winnowed their thrust. Before long, the moon would shrink behind them and then vanish completely from visual.

"You're looking good, *Altares*," Delta Control called over the radio. "Course confirmed."

Masters approved of Delta's praise. More so, he acknowledged the launch's success by how right the ship felt beneath him. *Smooth sailing*, he thought. Smoother than he'd anticipated. Better than she'd performed on her two shakedown cruises through the inner solar system as far as the Earth-facing side of wobbling Mercury and as far into the outer reaches of Sol to a swing around Neptune's moon Triton. What was to follow would be the true test of the light ship's success.

"*Altares* on course," Bowen reported from the Navigation Area.

Masters tipped a look to his right. "Rotate the particle scoop on 317."

Jane reached toward the proper lever and carried out the order. Masters imagined the vane projecting up from the topside of *Altares'* superstructure responding, taking aim, and rotating to carry out its all-important function of seizing onto the limitless fuel that powered their main engine.

"Three one seven," Jane confirmed.

And here it was, Masters thought. The

words seemed to take their time in reaching his lips, as though the leap forward through space soon to come had slowed them.

"Activating Photon Drive," he eventually managed.

He reached toward the controls. The sluggish spell continued, adding long seconds to the act. Masters realized the hesitation wasn't entirely in his mind, but the result of their incredible momentum, about to increase to many times the speed they'd already attained. Masters focused. He pressed the button.

At their backs, lights lit on the Photon Drive Chamber's door. The RADIO-ACTIVE protocol flashed in bold red letters. An alarm klaxon accompanied, singing out a warning of what was to follow.

The light ship's main engine activated. Inside *Altares*, the raw, pure power building toward release in the star drive doubled, quadrupled, rumbling around and through her crew.

"Standby," said Masters.

In the Navigation Area, both David and Bowen tensed in their seats. Farther behind, Anna gripped the sides of the medical couch, her eyes tightly shut. The siren continued its warning.

The Photon Drive engaged in a blinding, white-hot effulgence.

Altares raced forward.

Chapter Four

The light ship accelerated.

Velocity readings on the gage above Master's chair scrolled steadily faster—one glance, and they were cutting over a hundred thousand miles and change per second. Their momentum thrust his spine against the seat's back. Masters looked again. 149,950. The gage read past the 150,000 mile per second mark before he glanced an inch higher, at that all-important holiest of holy truths spelled out on the panel: MAX SPEED 186,000 MILES PER SECOND.

They weren't there yet, but nearing as the velocity meter's numbers sped into a blur.

The air grew heavier. Bowen rolled his eyes to his left and saw David struggling for breath. He imagined the same held true for Anna in the Monitoring Area and attempted to turn around in his chair. The gravitational forces ramping up inside *Altares* refused to allow it.

This was what was expected, and how things had to be. The light ship trembled around them, and the weight pressing against Bowen's chest doubled. But the air didn't clot, and *Altares* held her structural integrity. His next sip of breath proved to be less of a struggle.

Almost there, Bowen thought. They'd soon reach maximum velocity. Evidence of that fact was displayed on their screens, of *Altares* as captured by Delta's long-range eyes. The light ship glowed a vibrant red.

"You're still looking great, *Altares*," Forbes called over the intercom. "Acceleration effect is as predicted."

Pilot and copilot struggled to look up at the big screen, at the fleeting image projected from the space station.

"You're well into the red spectrum of the Doppler Shift."

Faster. Faster yet.

Masters knew what was sure to follow — that state where their increasing speed would test the limits of the human body. The discomfort started on his inside, a tickle that grew, helped along by backbone held rigid against seat and their building flirtation with reaching the speed of light. The caresses spread outward, engulfing his body in a sensation he remembered from that long test flight to Neptune — what his imagination translated into the pins and needles of limbs that had fallen asleep. Only this time, it slithered all over, inside his anatomy as well as outside.

And the malaise wasn't only confined to his imagination. No, it manifested physically in waves of force that gossiped across flesh. It swayed over the skin of cheeks and knuckles, as though intending to rip epidermis from muscles, skeleton. The discomfort ramped up to actual pain, the kind that traveled deeper than blood or marrow, all the way to the fabric of the soul.

Masters fought against the growing agony, which pushed his lips back from his teeth and attempted to drive his cheeks into his eye sockets. *Altares* fared no better, and seemed to cave in around them.

"I know you're all under severe 'g' force stress," Controller Forbes said over the radio. "But if you look at your screens, you'll see the illusion of the *Altares* being crushed up is exactly as Einstein predicted."

Masters rolled his gaze up to the screen. He recognized the red glow, and the mirage that the light ship was folding in upon herself, a modern, massive version of the legendary Ouroboros, the mythological serpent depicted devouring its own tail.

But there was something else, more— there, on the velocity readout, for an instant, maybe a fraction of a second, the figures didn't make sense. Their speed had jumped above the maximum spelled out by the numbers on top.

The wheels turned another tenth of a rotation before dialing back down to match the speed of light.

Still, Masters felt it, a churning in his guts, his blood, his soul: the certainty that *Altares* would crunch in upon herself, Ouroboros cannibalizing itself completely. He rolled his eyes to the right, terrified that Jane would be gone along with that side of the light ship. His daughter's frail form was pressed back against the copilot's chair.

"We're losing you," said Forbes.

Fear jolted through Masters, because the pressure tearing them up was about to puncture *Altares*' hull, turning her inside out in the vacuum of space. They would crunch up only to then come apart in a spectacular shower of debris, all of it colored red at first. No, he told himself. It was unforgivable to think of their end so soon after taking off from Delta.

He struggled to speak Jane's name, but the lone word died before reaching his lips.

"We're losing linkup," Forbes said in a voice that sounded as though it originated from the other side of the galaxy. "Goodbye, *Altares*."

The link cut out, and the radio went silent. The unpleasant caresses over skin continued. Masters assumed the same painful ripples were taking place in the Navigation Area with Bowen and the boy. Farther back, too, plaguing Anna. He hadn't remembered the stress being this bad before, the pressure so crushing. Enough to compact *Altares*.

Masters' thoughts mirrored the Controller's final words. *Goodbye, Altares.*

A sound crackled in his head — a kind of white noise set in counterpoint above the building chorus bottled inside the light ship. That, Masters remembered from his previous accelerations through Earth's solar system. It was, he agreed, a kind of balancing out — the human brain adjusting to forces it had not been designed to experience.

As had happened during those other flights, the teakettle whistle around him crescendoed, and the ripple effect stopped feasting upon his flesh. Another glance at the velocity counter showed their speed had attained an impressive mark and was still climbing. Proof was all around them as the *Altares* quaked, her superstructure intact despite the illusions of false endings that filled view screens.

Past the 175,268 mile per second mark now, Masters saw. But hadn't they, even for an instant, traveled even *faster*, according to the counter? He'd misread the velocity gage, surely, when the stress was doing its best to flatten his eyeballs in their sockets. Faster than light was impossible; no matter what the terrible unease in his gut attempted to prove. And that evidence, weak for the argument as it was, had started to thin out, evaporating like the mad pressure and pulses that kept them static in their seats.

The Photon Drive main propulsion rocket flared with an eruption of blue-white light before switching off and going dark. 178,141 mps, according to the velocity gage.

Altares raced onward at just under the speed of light.

The frenetic klaxon from the Chamber cut out, taking most of the noise with it. *Altares* was intact and moving at incredible speed, headed on course and toward her intended destination.

A trick of the eye, that's all, Masters thought. *I only imagined it.*

The pressure inside the light ship abated.

All was well.

Masters released the safety harness and sat up. The rush on the other side of accelerating the light ship almost to her max speed exhilarated him. He turned to Jane and saw she'd already unbuckled from her straps.

"All right?" he asked.

Jane nodded. "The acceleration nearly flattened me!"

He could imagine, given how the stress had affected his own anatomy. "Well, we had some pretty hectic forces working on us."

Masters checked the instruments in front of them. Everything looked satisfactory — as good as when *Altares* was levitating above Delta Station in readiness to launch, not cutting past the inner solar system and into the outer reaches of Sol.

Jane assisted in evaluating their status from the copilot's seat. "I know it was just an illusion, but wasn't it scary when the space cameras showed *Altares* crushing up?"

Scary? There had been a moment when he'd been afraid and he'd thought the impossible had happened. "Only if you suffer from too much imagination," he said, and sold himself on the notion that the lie was for Jane's benefit and not his. "What does computer say?"

"You mean about Einstein's Theory of Space Contraction?"

He saw the slightest smile playing on Jane's mouth, a thing barely there. "No, the ship."

"Oh, the ship," she teased. "All systems fine, Captain."

"Thank you," he fired back.

Jane gave the board another quick scan. "Looks like we're on our way."

Bowen unbuckled his safety harness and sucked in a deep breath. The ache in his chest waned. The one in his molars persisted. He realized he was still grinding his teeth and willed his jaws to relax.

The stress of accelerating to near-light speed appeared less taxing on David. His son was already up from their station at the chart table, checking and rechecking their course at the navigational computer station.

"Point-five degree error?" David asked.

Bowen examined the readings on the chart table. Pride for his son rose up within him, a warmth that dispelled the lingering chill. "You're right." Then, in a louder voice, he passed the information up to the Flight Deck. "Skipper, we gained a point-five degree error on launch."

Masters absorbed the report. Point-five degrees difference could easily be explained on any number of factors, not the least of which was their rapid leap to such fantastic speeds. So why did his insides tighten up again?

"Compute corrections and feed them in, Tom," Masters said.

An easy fix, one that Bowen managed with the flip of a few buttons. *All systems fine*, Jane had said.

Masters settled back in his chair and tried to believe it.

Chapter Five

Altares cut across space.

David poured over images displayed on the chart table. Jane ambled past his station and approached the Navigation Area's direct vision porthole. At their starboard, a small planet materialized. Five moons ringed the frigid dwarf, which shone a bright cobalt color beyond the glass.

"There's a blue planet coming up to us now," she said.

David left the star charts and joined her at the space window. The dwarf planet glowed under the scraps of light cast by distant Sol. It was there at that moment but would be gone in the next as the Photon Drive sped them past.

"It's Pluto, and it's not blue," David said. "We're traveling so fast that the light waves are squashed up to the short end of the spectrum. So it only *looks* blue."

Jane blinked. Pluto was already fading from view, its color altering.

"As it recedes," David continued on the swing back to his station. "You'll see it turn red. It's called the Doppler Shift."

"Navigators," Jane said lightly. "You think you know it all."

David tipped a glance in the direction of the porthole. "Just enough to get us where we're going."

Jane cast a final look at the dwarf planet, now shrinking at their backs. The vibrant blue was gone, replaced by a red that was equally intense. "Goodbye, Pluto," she said. "Goodbye, solar system."

The red planet dimmed.

Altares charged on.

The steady vibrations from the light ship's velocity trembled up through the deck plates, past the soles of Anna's sneakers, and into her bones.

You're riding at the front of a comet, her inner voice taunted. *Sol's four gas giants are at your back now. You're in the Kuiper Belt, beyond Neptune. Soon, you'll exit the solar system. You're a long way from Earth. From him.*

She glided out of the Monitoring Area, into Navigation. Bowen and David were working, likely maintaining the ship's course while also making sure *Altares* didn't intersect with any of the Kuiper Belt's asteroids. While most of the inner solar system's space refuse was comprised of rock or metal, those in this region past Neptune were composed mostly of frozen volatiles — ammonia, methane, and water. They were just as dangerous, but nothing that the light ship's forward laser cannon couldn't eliminate should they fly too close.

"Time for stress checks," Anna said. "You first, David."

Her son stabbed at buttons and passed on the entirety of navigation duties to Bowen. "Right," he said. Then David hastened into the Monitoring Area.

Anna hesitated from following. Instead, she approached her husband. "Hi."

"Hi," Bowen answered.

He flashed one of those rare smiles, but the gesture barely warmed her. "How was David?"

Bowen's smile widened at the mention of their son, and Anna remembered how attractive she'd once found his happiness, especially when it resulted from her. "Just fine. It won't be long before he makes me obsolete around here."

"I'll remember that."

She glanced away and turned back in the direction of the Monitoring Area. *Altares* was massive, a juggernaut in scope, true. But most of her mass was devoted to engines and other life support mech — the amount of space available to her crew being the least of her components. It was good that the ice between them had started to melt, given their close living accommodations.

David stood waiting before the opaque bio-telemetry panel. Anna clipped the monitor's leads to three points on the chest of his uniform and tapped buttons, activating the medical device.

"How do you feel?" she asked.

David tensed noticeably. "Still a bit light in the head."

"Who are you kidding? You've always been like that."

The boy grinned. "I must have been to come on this trip."

Anna brushed a stray lock of hair out of her son's eyes. David pulled away from her fingers.

"Hold still."

She pressed a switch. The telemetry panel lit, its surface showing a three-dimensional map of David's body beneath the skin. In real time, heart pumped blood. Lungs expanded with breaths and contracted from exhales. Monitors on the panel recorded blood pressure, blood oxygen count, pulse rate, and body temperature. Everything looked mostly normal.

"Mother," David said.

Anna looked up from her clipboard. "Yes?"

"Did you feel something, after the Photon Drive activated?"

She had—a lot of crushing pressure and

noise, and told him so. "Is that what you mean?"

"Yes, but there was something more to it. It felt as though one second I was sitting there at my station, and the next I was in a dark place. A room with no light, no air. I was in severe pain. That's the best way I can explain it."

Anna remembered hiding behind her closed eyes. "According to our pilot and Chief Navigator, the launch went off without a hitch."

David shook his head. "No, that isn't true. The course variation. It's acceptable, given our speed, but *Altares* is better than that. More, so is Dad."

Anna removed the leads. "Taking a ride on the Photon Drive was scary."

"I wasn't scared."

"All right, then—*exhilarating*. None of the computers or specialists aboard have detected anything wrong, though I doubt your father would object to you reviewing our flight data. Now, go on with you."

David straightened his jacket but remained standing in front of the screen. "Mother, do you think we'll ever find other forms of life out here in space?"

Anna answered while saving the bio-telemetry data to the computer. "Statistically, there's no doubt about it."

"It would be very different from ours, wouldn't it?"

"Well, yes, life does evolve to suit the conditions of its own particular solar system. But different or not, we could still learn from it."

"Learn…how? It'd be alien to us."

"Maybe. But certain things are basic to all life forms," Anna said. "The most important, I suppose, is survival, something we on Earth have not been all that good at."

David sighed. "You mean the destruction of our environment and our natural resources, pollution. Things like that?"

"Our record hasn't been all that impressive, has it?"

"I suppose not," he answered before looking around at the inner walls of the Monitoring Area. "However, see where we are, on this ship, sailing farther and faster away from Delta, a city built in space." David drank down a sip of breath. "There is one question though we're not going to find the answer to, not even out here."

"Only one?" Anna said wryly.

"Yes, the big one. Where it all came from — life, the universe, everything."

"No, David, I don't suppose we will." She switched off the bio-telemetry panel.

"How am I doing?"

"You'll survive. Tell your father he's next."

David nodded. "Yes, Doctor."

David spotted the meteorite swarm on the light ship's long distance eyes before the computer raised the alarm. More debris from the

Oort Cloud to be avoided. He moved quickly from the instruments to the chart table and made his calculations.

"Captain," he called. "Course alteration...seven degrees to port."

Masters acknowledged. "Seven degrees port. What's up?"

"Unidentified objects ahead. Probably a meteorite shower," David answered.

Altares easily made her course corrections. Ahead of her, the deadly objects glinted like fireflies at night, tumbling through the darkness beyond Earth's solar system.

The alarm continued its bleat, warning of the swarm's proximity. Jane returned to the porthole. The meteorites came into view, reflecting what little of Sol's light reached this far out. Their sparkle reminded her of precious gemstones.

"They're beautiful," she said.

"And dangerous," said David. "If one of those hit us, we wouldn't even know it."

Jane turned away from the porthole and approached the chart table. "David, if everything goes well and we get to Alpha Centauri, would you really want to go farther?"

The boy ceased working. "Well, I told the selection board I did."

"You haven't answered my question."

He aimed his eyes ahead of the Navigation Area, into the cockpit. Jane tracked them to the forward space window set before the pilot's and copilot's chairs. "Yes, I do want to know what's out here in space. Just imagine, there are something like a million Earth-type planets in the Milky Way alone. Sometime, I'd like to land on just one of them."

David faced her.

"And you?"

"I think I'd like to go back to Earth before it changes too much. I mean, thirty years is a long time, isn't it?"

David nodded and suddenly felt cold. In the shutter-clicks between blinks, his memory traveled back to that fraction of a second when he'd found himself trapped inside a dark room, paralyzed by fear, agony, and struggling to breathe. His arms broke in gooseflesh beneath the covering of his jacket.. Wide-eyed, he looked around the ship, at first not believing his own eyes.

"What's wrong?" Jane asked.

The answer eluded him, except for the certainty that whatever had happened to them during *Altares'* acceleration away from Earth was real.

Chapter Six

The ship sailed on course toward her destination, surrounded on all sides by a thousand distant stars. Many of those points of light appeared on the chart table's screen, freshly captured by *Altares'* cameras. Bowen stored the new images into the system, fodder for an untold number of future manned missions by those who followed.

In front of him, Masters stirred. Bowen looked up to see their captain climb out of the pilot's seat.

"Time for a bit of shut eye?" he asked.

Masters nodded. Bowen left the chart table and approached the vacated pilot's controls.

"She's on automatic," Masters said. "I'd leave her that way."

Bowen took the chair. "You don't trust

me?"

"In a word…no!"

Both men exchanged a good-natured laugh. Masters continued through to the Navigation Area, where David conducted the important work of recording and cataloguing images at the chart table.

"Still know where we are?" he asked the boy.

David pressed a switch. A high-res image of a luminous blue variable star materialized on the table's screen, its clarity stunning.

"Sailors in the old days really had it easy. They were always looking at the same old sky."

"Just think," Masters said. "You're the first sailor to see this new sky."

David smiled. "To answer your question, yes, we know where we are. And just in case we get lost…"

He activated a switch. A reassuring melody poured forth from the light ship's long-range receivers.

"We're still picking up Delta Beacon," David said.

Masters patted the boy's shoulder on his way past to the Crew's Quarters. He climbed into the upper bunk located above the one where Jane lay, already fast asleep.

They were accelerating again, and Jane was convinced the stressful forces would crush her. Simulations at Spaceport Beta and the training mission through the inner and outer planets hadn't prepared her for the reality of flight using the Photon Drive.

"*Jane*," the disembodied voice whispered.

The misery was at its worst, the voice a manifestation, a memory knocked loose by the jolts as *Altares* threatened to shake herself apart. Only it came a second time.

"*Jane!*"

The stresses abated, and when Jane blinked, the crushing weight was off her chest. According to the view past the direct vision port, *Altares* was still racing ahead at fantastic speed, just beneath that of light. She tipped a glance at the velocity gage. For a second, the readout made no sense—it had gone *past* the speed of light! No, *Altares* wasn't designed to exceed the standard. Their maximum velocity was—

The lights cut out. Not just those illuminating the inside of the Flight Deck, but all of the telltales and ambient glows from computer screens and instrument panels. The ship continued her charge through space, only that, too, was different. It felt as though they were coasting now, a giant metal stone skipping across the biggest pond imaginable. As soon as the momentum ran out, *Altares* would sink.

Cold fear slithered across Jane's skin. She lifted from the copilot's chair and saw that the pilot's seat was empty. Struggling to find her voice, she said, "Dad?"

No answer came. Jane turned toward the

Navigation Area. As though on cue, all of the lights in that section of the ship winked out. The Monitoring Area and Crew's Quarters followed, leaving *Altares* bathed in darkness except for the warning lights that marked the Photon Drive.

"Hello?" Jane called out in a trembling voice.

No one answered. The invisible ice forming over her skin thickened. She was alone, and the light ship was spiraling off course, with nobody to correct its trajectory or stop it from colliding with any number of objects, planets, or stars.

"We made it back to Earth, Jane," the voice said.

In the absence of sound and the darkness filling *Altares*, Jane heard it clearly, understood that it was a woman's voice, though burbled and not sounding entirely human. She tracked it into the Photon Drive Chamber, to the reinforced door just past the heat and radiation barriers. Movement, a shadow—

"Oh yes, we returned, Jane."

The figure stepped closer, and despite the surrounding darkness, Jane saw that it, like the voice, wasn't fully human in definition but distorted. The shadow-thing approached. Jane shook her head and matched its advance toward her with an equal number of steps back-peddled in retreat. The copilot's chair stopped her from going any farther.

"And do you know what happened

next?" the figure asked. "What became of our dear Mother?"

The shadow was in the Navigation Area now. Jane spun around. There wasn't anywhere left to go. The space between pilot's chair and the direct vision window offered a yard at most. But the image through the reinforced glass stopped her where she stood. Beyond the spiraling *Altares* was a desolate planet stripped of its cloud cover and also its oceans. The craggy wasteland was still recognizable, given the familiar landmarks of the British Isles, Italy's boot, and the top third of the African continent.

From the curve of the dead planet, another feature rose up. A space station, Jane thought, even as her heart threatened to explode in her chest and the seconds dragged on. The massive construct swam into clear view. It was vaster and more streamlined than Delta, the new Epsilon Space Station, or anything else that had been fashioned in orbit around the Earth. Larger than any of the cities built or planned for the lunar surface, too. Through her panic, Jane identified the construct's shape as being that of a pair of parallel helices intertwined around a shared axis.

"Double helix," she gasped.

"That's right, Jane," the shadow said, suddenly so close that Jane felt the stirring of foul breath across the nape of her neck.

The face belonging to that voice reflected in the space window.

"Take a good look at what you did!"

Impossible. *Inhuman*. Jane only saw the twisted visage for a fraction of a second before *Altares* ended skipping across space and was plummeting down, down, toward what promised to be a fiery impact with the dead planet. But the brief glimpse was enough.

Jane screamed.

And screamed.

She jolted awake and managed to trap the shriek powering up from her guts behind her teeth. The Crew's Quarters. Lights were dimmed but still active. The terrible sensation of being flung out of control dulled; *Altares* was flying fast and steady according to the vibrations echoing up through the deck. A dream, that's all it was. One of the worst of her life.

Jane passed a hand over her face. She was soaked in clammy sweat. Her heart continued its mad gallop, despite the proof offered by her eyes. A nightmare, nothing more. She shouldn't have been surprised, given what had happened to her as the light ship powered up to breakneck speed. The pressure had tried its best to kill them.

She exhaled and settled back on the bunk. The hideous image of that face in reflection materialized before her, projected onto the gray canvas of the Crew's Quarters. Then she remembered Winnie, and fished the snowflake tag out of her jacket pocket and held it tightly, like a talisman.

While David slept, Bowen worked at the chart table amassing data and scanning for objects in their path. He picked at the selection of rations on the small plastic tray—nothing that tasted overly appealing or actually filled him up, but he'd grown used to that, as he had his wife's distance.

Anna. Bowen set down the sextant and turned from the breathtaking imagery of mysterious stars seen only from great distances before the *Altares* Mission. He glanced into the Crew's Quarters, where Anna and David rested. On the surface, his relationship with his wife seemed fine, and had been for all those cameras and throughout the many interviews before departing Earth. They were cordial with one another, and her smile, which she often blessed him with, still inspired his in like. But he knew something was different. *Absent*, was how he privately described it.

He reached for another handful of crumble that mixed together freeze-dried fruits, vegetables, nuts, and a salty dusting of high protein powder. No, it wasn't particularly satisfying but it sustained him.

Bowen turned back to the charts. Images scrolled past—still shots from recent captures by the ship's cameras. The automated review cut out and switched over to live feed. Projected onto the screen was a bright cluster of nearby stars set against a backdrop of black velvet

dotted by silver. Two words accompanied the study.
Alpha Centauri.

Altares' Photon Drive fired in reverse thrust, and the light ship decelerated. The massive metal arrow slowed to a stop. Ahead, the star cluster blazed, Alpha Centauri A and its binary mate, Alpha Centauri B. The third star in the cluster, the faint dwarf Proxima Centauri, glowed red among its peers.

Jane stared out the porthole. Squinting, she could just make out the system's lone planet, a rocky world slightly larger than the Earth called Alpha Centauri Bb for the star it orbited. The view was beautiful and filled her with emotion.

Masters cut around the Navigation Area and joined her at the porthole. "Excuse me, Ma'am, but do you work here or are you just window shopping?"

Jane chuckled at her father's joke, which felt good. She couldn't remember the last time she'd laughed. The reprieve was short-lived.

"We've arrived," he said. "We're here." Then Masters turned to Bowen. "Tom, contact Earth. Tell them...tell them we've made it!"

Bowen vacated his seat at the chart table and moved to the light ship's radio transmitter. It would be a long while before anyone back home heard the news. Still, he shared in the general excitement building around them.

"Space Station Delta," Bowen broadcast. "This is the *Altares*. We are safe and well and have reached our first objective...*Alpha Centauri!*"

Chapter Seven

They worked together as a team, mostly in silence. David stood before the computer terminal, feeding instructions. Masters manned the controls. The two exchanged a look.

"Ready," David said.

Masters keyed in his authorization code and pressed the last button. *Altares* barely trembled, just enough that her captain felt it.

The first of the hangar doors trundled open beneath the massive Directional Antenna. The satellite fired its thrusters and rolled free of the light ship, aimed toward the trinary star group. Its beacon pinged a signal back to their receivers.

"And we're green," David said. "First satellite deployed. She's moving into position and transmitting on full power."

Masters flashed a thumbs-up to his young

assistant as the signal played through the ship, nearly musical in its repetition.

It was, Anna thought, a kind of celebration. She stowed the container of interstellar dust harvested soon after their arrival to Alpha Centauri among other samples gathered along the way. A celebration, yes. She caught herself smiling and jotted down time and date in the computer's catalog.

Altares quivered around them again. The second satellite exited the light ship, following its predecessor out into the Alpha Centauri system.

Bowen glanced up from the chart table, which was trained on the three stars and their lone rocky planet. It was good to see David so engaged in the work. More than an assignment, his son had taken to the mission as though it were a calling. Whatever reservations he'd once suffered over pulling his family so far from home were gone. To have denied his son the opportunities afforded by the *Altares* would have been criminal.

The third satellite floated free of the hanger. Once clear of the light ship's superstructure, its boosters engaged and it began to maneuver away. At minimum safe distance, Satellite 3 extended its eyes and ears—a trio of powerful broadcasting arrays, one aimed at Earth, one linked to *Altares*, the other at the vast unknown spread out before them.

"All satellites online," David said.

The proof of that claim could be heard in the triple melody pinging through *Altares*.

"It's lovely," Jane said.

Masters agreed. "Music to my ears," he said, meaning the remark to sound light.

But as soon as the words were out, he regretted them. That reverberating beat meant the mission was accomplished, and that it was time to circle back in the direction of Earth.

Masters cast a glance around *Altares*, seeing Jane in the copilot's seat, keeping them at a steady distance from the trinary star cluster, Bowen mapping the region thanks to additional intelligence already streaming in from the satellite chain, David rapping up the last of the work on the satellites themselves. Now angled on course and settling into fixed orbits, the information sent back would prove vital for future expeditions to Alpha Centauri, including manned landings on Planet Bb, and beyond.

Beyond. That particular concept pulsed in Master's thoughts, echoing between the musical beats broadcast from the satellite chain. They could return or continue. Already, their time in deep space was creating a widening gap between the crew of *Altares* and the people back home. Still, the work they were doing was of immeasurable benefit to a world in jeopardy from pollution, overpopulation, and the squandering of natural resources. Masters sensed that to turn around now was a mistake.

Anna entered from the Monitoring Area,

clipboard in hand. "Good job, all."

Masters smiled. "Don't count yourself out of the praise, Anna. We've done it—and we're bang on schedule."

A new sound joined the computerized symphony, a prompt from the light ship's receivers. Tom moved from the chart table to the broadcast systems and killed the triple-ping.

"We're getting a signal from Satellite 3," he said.

Jane returned *Altares* to automatic pilot and joined the others around the screen. "From Earth?"

Bowen thumbed a sequence of buttons. "Yes. Standby for Earth linkup."

The receivers came to life, at first piping in a hollow sound, an emptiness. Then the familiar voice of Controller Forbes poured forth as clearly as if the man was standing with them in the Navigation Area.

"Hello *Altares*. This signal is traveling at the speed of light, and was transmitted one year after your departure from Earth," the man said. "Since your velocity is slightly less than 186,000 miles per second, it has been computed to catch up with you on completion of your work program in the vicinity of Alpha Centauri."

In that moment of heightened awareness, Masters saw Anna tense and turn away from the screen, clearly a reaction to hearing the Controller's voice. She quickly composed herself, which solidified his belief that something more was at play.

"The moment has now come for you to make a heartrending decision," Forbes continued. "Whether to return to Earth or move deeper into space to your second objective."

The screen lit, and Forbes appeared, his image distorted by snow. The storm blew away and the picture stabilized, showing Forbes in his crisp white uniform with its black stripes and collar.

"Whatever your decision is, all the nations of Earth will remember your achievements with pride and affection. Good luck to you all. End of Delta transmission."

The picture froze, with the Controller in the process of reaching for the button on his desk that would close the link. A long few seconds passed during which that hollow sound returned. Then the screen switched to its hibernation view, the live feed of Proxima Centauri sent back by the new satellite chain.

Masters risked another look at Anna Bowen. Whatever secret plagued her in silence was again safely hidden, and she'd composed herself behind an icy mask, if only barely. The ghost of emotions that had escaped, however briefly, still haunted her eyes and the corner of her mouth, which trembled. He thought he knew or could at least guess at the nature of her worries. The five crewmembers of the *Altares* Mission had traveled a long way together in fairly close quarters. He'd seen and felt the chill between Bowen and his wife. And also, his better angel reminded, their commitment to one another this far from Earth.

Whatever Anna knew with Controller Forbes, Masters figured that it was part of another life, one long ended and far behind them.

In the wake of the transmittal, the crew fell silent. Masters looked from one solemn face to another.

"Well, which is it to be? You know the rules—we all agreed to them on Delta. One dissenting voice and we return."

David was the first to volunteer his vote. "Forward."

Anna quickly answered, "I agree," and wiped at her eyes.

Or course she does, thought Masters. He sensed her pain, even shared it after a fashion. Had life treated him and Jane kinder, there might have been a crew of six aboard the light ship. Yes, he knew the crushing misery of losing the love of one's life, even if the situations were different.

Masters sent a smile in Anna's direction before facing their navigator. "Tom?"

"Count me in, Skipper," Bowen said.

Masters faced Jane. His daughter turned away from the others, burying her focus on the back of the nearest chair.

"Jane?"

She spun back wearing a brave face. "Yes,

let's go on," she said, though Masters guessed the decision wasn't her first choice.

His vote made it unanimous. "Okay, we go on."

He rounded Jane, cut through the Navigation Area, and entered the Flight Deck. Masters returned with a long, narrow cylinder. Instead of colorful interstellar dust, crystal fragments, or other matter samples collected between Sol and Alpha Centauri, this sample case contained a scroll of parchment paper.

Masters opened the scroll and read what was written.

"We, the people from the planet Earth, the first to escape from their solar system, wish to commemorate this historic occasion by placing this document in a small satellite, which will now become part of the Alpha Centauri solar system for all time. Signed, Captain Harry Masters, *Altares*."

Jane placed her hand on the cylinder. "And Cadet Jane Masters."

David joined them. "Cadet David Bowen."

"Space scientist Anna Bowen."

Bowen was the last to lay his hand on the cylinder. "Navigator Tom Bowen."

"Amen," Jane said. "So be it."

Masters liked that.

He rolled up the document and returned it to the cylinder. "David, you up for one more satellite launch today?"

"Yes, Captain," the boy said.

The fourth satellite was considerably smaller than its predecessors. Satellite 4 boosted away from *Altares* and chased the paths of the others in the chain.

Countdown to launch commenced. Soon, the Photon Drive would activate and propel them at crushing speeds out of the Alpha Centauri system, toward their next mission objective. The small, symbolic dinner was nearly finished when the radio chirped.

Masters glanced up from his tray. "What's that?"

Bowen stood and crossed the Crew's Quarters and Monitoring Area. In Navigation, he approached a lit green telltale at the wall of instruments. "Incoming signal," he said.

Masters and the rest of the crew followed in.

"More time-delayed well wishes from Earth?"

Bowen shook his head. "No, Skipper. This is coming in during actual time…and from much closer."

"Where?" Masters asked.

Bowen checked figures. "It's being bounced back from one of our new satellites — from Orbital Reference Point 3-1-1."

"From Alpha Centauri?" asked Jane.

"Proxima Centauri, to be precise," Bowen said. All emotion ironed off his face. "Could it be a signal from some higher form of intelligent alien life?"

"Let's find out," said Masters. "Open the channel."

Bowen thumbed the switch. *Altares'* radio receivers activated.

"Hello?" said Masters. "This is the captain of the Earth light ship *Altares*. Do you read us?"

A cold silence answered.

Chapter Eight

It was the empty breeze of the void, Jane thought, even as her arms blossomed in gooseflesh beneath the protective warmth of her regulation uniform jacket.

Only it proved to be not as empty as she first believed. A click sounded over the link. Another followed, and then a voice, one that sounded as though it originated from the farthest end of the universe.

"*Croatoan*," it said. Female, deep.

A shiver teased the nape of Jane's neck. She fought it, failed. The chill tumbled.

Masters looked around at faces and saw that all were frozen in place by the connection to whoever was at the other end of that transmission. Moving took conscious effort. He ordered his body to thaw and pressed down on the microphone. "I repeat, this is Harry Masters, captain of *Altares*. Please identify."

Another series of clicks followed, and then the signal cut out.

Masters stepped away from the equipment. "Get them back, Tom!"

Bowen replaced Masters at the radio. He ran through the expected broadcast procedure. "Let me state for the record," he said, "that I am following communications protocol set forth by the Space Authority on the chance that *Altares* Mission encounters alien intelligence."

"Duly noted," Masters said. "Now, Tom-?"

"On it, Skipper."

While Bowen attempted to reestablish contact, David had cast off his frost and was at the chart table, working the light ship's Directional Antenna. The powerful broadcast dish rising up from the topside of *Altares'* superstructure swiveled in compliance.

"I've got it," David exclaimed. "Contact and location of the source of that transmission!"

The chart table displayed the trinary stars, with a graph superimposed over the live feed.

"There," David said.

He aimed his pointer finger at the red dwarf star, and a coordinate almost occluded by its intense corona.

"Can you get us visual?" Masters asked.

"I'll try," David said.

The radio was picking up more of that dead space dirge. Masters caught himself pacing between the bank of instruments and the chart table. Stopping himself, he faced his copilot.

"Jane, prepare to take *Altares* in on sublight engines," he said.

Whatever melancholy she'd suffered over the decision to move deeper into unexplored space instead of returning to home soil was gone. Jane hastened into the Flight Deck and strapped into her chair.

"Sending coordinates," David said.

"Got them," Jane answered. "Plotting course."

Masters started toward the pilot's chair, only to stop at the sight of Anna, standing alone, haunted both by the specter of Forbes and whatever it was much closer at the nearby red dwarf star. He cut a line toward her and set both hands on her shoulders. Anna jolted in place.

"You'd better strap in," he said.

Anna forced a smile. "Yes."

"But be ready just in case there's something and someone out there. You're not just our doctor, you're the closest thing to a diplomat we've got."

Anna nodded. Masters released her and continued to the Flight Deck.

"I've got something," David said at his back. "Putting it on the main screen, Captain."

The picture on the monitor above their heads altered from the trinary cluster to show only the red dwarf star. Their view neared as the light ship's cameras zoomed in, and neared again. By the third adjustment, a solid red field covered the screen, the glow almost too intense to look upon for more than a few seconds. Masters narrowed his eyes. His imagination translated the image into blood, stretching from one side of the monitor to the other.

"Firing steering rockets and ready on your order," Jane said. "I have us on a high orbital path matching the course of our satellites to avoid the star's corona."

"Execute," Masters said.

Steering rockets fired, turning the light ship's prow toward Proxima Centauri. The chemical rockets followed, repeating that dazzling geyser-pyrotechnics display that had originally boosted them away from Space Station Delta and the Earth. The light ship's stationary reprieve ended. She resumed moving and picked up speed. The blood red glow of their unexpected new course streamed in through the space windows and bathed the cockpit. The dwarf star's light pooled around them, making it impossible for Masters to shake the analogy.

"Course correction," Bowen called.

Masters made the adjustment. A pull-down window on the main screen tracked their heading. "Done. Tom, anything else from our mysterious friends?"

"No, Skipper. Maybe they're shy."

David called their attention back to the screen. "*There!*"

The grid reappeared over the sea of red light. In the upper left corner of the screen, one square flashed, drawing their attention. Masters looked into the effulgence. Hanging against that vast puddle of luminous blood, he just made out a shape, dark and inelegant. Slitting his eyelids didn't help. The red dwarf's glare stung at his retinas.

"*Altares* on approach," Jane said.

"Captain, object is on the move," David called from Navigation.

Masters blinked. In the fraction of a second between the shutter-click, the dark mass was gone from the grid. David's trackers followed it into the square above; no longer set against the red backdrop, visual became impossible.

"We're losing contact," David said. "Object is falling behind the star."

In another second, it was gone completely from eyes and instruments.

"Do we pursue?" Jane asked.

Masters nodded. "We have to."

Altares continued her charge toward Proxima Centauri.

The light ship braked and held position to starboard of their new satellite network.

"Nothing," David sighed. "Whoever they were, they're gone."

"Why wouldn't they talk with us?" asked Jane.

Frustrated, Masters sighed. "I don't know. But I'm confident now in saying the question of whether or not we're alone out here has been answered."

He cast a glance at the screen, where the static image of the dark mass set against the canvas of the red star was projected.

Anna marched in from the Monitoring Area. "Permission to activate the scoop, Captain."

Masters drew in a deep breath. "More interstellar dust?"

"Yes, and no," Anna said. "There's a particulate trail along the course that object took. It could give us insight into the nature of our new friends."

Masters gave Anna his blessing. She moved to the scoop controls, and adjusted the settings from photon collection to the material she'd spotted on the ship's scanners.

"It's a damn mystery," Masters sighed.

David looked up from the chart table's screen. "We've got another one, sir."

Masters and Jane approached his station. "What have you found?"

"The alien craft—if that's what it was— signaled us through the new network of satellites we launched to aid future missions and to bolster our connection with Earth."

"Sure," Masters said.

"I just scanned the satellites—all three are functioning at optimum. But the fourth, the one we launched before that ship made contact…I can't find it."

"Our message in a bottle?" Jane asked.

"It's gone," David said. "I've checked and rechecked the scanners and it's nowhere to be found."

A level of silence crept through *Altares* in which only the ship's instruments spoke. After making another report to the Space Authority that wouldn't reach Earth for years, Masters focused on resuming their journey to their next objective beyond Alpha Centauri. Only one thing delayed them from leaving the star system.

Masters checked the clock.

"Course plotted," Jane said from his right. "We're ready to go as soon as you give the word, Dad."

Masters faced Jane. His growing frustration shorted out. Her hopeful smile brought him back from the confusion and disappointment following their strange encounter.

"Are you sure?" he asked in a voice meant only for her. "I mean, about going on, not returning to Earth."

"Aren't you?"

Until the garbled message came in, he had been. Before he could answer, the cadence of approaching footsteps alerted them that Anna was done with her analysis. Masters stood.

"I have my initial findings," Anna said

from the arch between the Flight Deck and Navigation. "The particulate matter is a mix of trace metal alloys and carbon residue."

"Alloys—then we are dealing with some form of manufactured space vehicle," Bowen said.

Masters could tell by her expression that the answer wasn't so easy to give. "The residue I collected is in a severe state of decay. In the few seconds it's taken me to reach the Navigation Area, the samples have likely degraded to the equivalent of dust."

"From exposure to our atmosphere?" Masters posed.

"No," Anna said. "My opinion as both a doctor and space sciences specialist is that what we collected from our mysterious visitors is more like skin. A kind of epidermis that covers their hull, shed the way our bodies dispose of dead skin cells."

More silence followed the revelation.

"How is that possible?" Bowen eventually asked.

Anna sighed a humorless chuckle through her nostrils. "I wish we could talk with them and find out."

"But they're gone," Masters said. "And now, I think it's our turn. Let's get out of here."

Chapter Nine

The Photon Drive activated. *Altares* propelled forward, her speed doubling, quadrupling. Crushing weight built with her velocity. In seconds, the trinary stars of Alpha Centauri glowing at their aft dimmed. Not long after that, the cluster had blurred into the background map of stars, and *Altares* was arrowing through the void between solar systems.

The light ship shot on, through that emptiness. More space debris appeared on the long-range scanners. Bowen adjusted their heading. New stars rose ahead of their bow.

"We're entering the gravitational field of the nearest stars," Bowen said.

Altares' controls wriggled in Masters' grasp, confirming the navigator's claim. "Switching to computer guidance system." He thumbed the proper switch. The noticeable trembling eased. "*Altares* now under automated computer guidance."

Bowen turned to David. "Are we holding course?"

David checked before answering. "Course stable."

The lights visible through the space window brightened as *Altares* charged closer. Masters looked out at the stellar bestiary they'd soon fly into.

"There are double- and triple-star systems inside that cluster, so hang on," he said. "We could be in for some gravitational turbulence."

The light ship raced into the cluster. One of those stars, a dim pinpoint seconds earlier, seemed to jump toward them, an optical illusion created by their impressive velocity. The star's glare intensified. So, too, did its pull. *Altares* banked to her port side, giving credence to the captain's warning.

Anna rocked with the ship and steadied herself at the arch between compartments. Now in the Flight Deck, she made it over to the view port. Outside, the nearby yellow star exerting its pull appeared to inflate. Half a dozen more stars jumped out of the cluster and into visual range.

Altares leveled out.

"Course still holding?" Masters asked.

Bowen double-checked. "Computer's happy."

Altares lurched again, this time to

starboard. Bowen glanced to his left and realized David was enjoying the bumpy ride. For all his son's intellect and maturity, he was reminded that David was still a boy.

The glare from the yellow sun died as *Altares* rocketed past. New stars replaced it, none so vibrant.

"Those suns," said Jane. "I know we're traveling close to them, yet they look so small."

"Some of them are larger than our own sun," Masters said. "It's our relative velocity that's shrinking them up."

Anna chose that moment to leave the porthole. She leaned over the back of Jane's chair. "Just as Einstein predicted."

"What a genius he was," Jane said. "He predicted all this even before we'd learned how to fly, let alone travel through space."

"All his work up until now was just theory, yet out here, seeing things behave exactly as he predicted, it's really something, isn't it, Harry?"

Masters agreed.

"Anna, was his Theory of Relativity his life's work?"

Anna faced the space window. "It was just a small part of it. He spent the last twenty years of his life in America, working on an even more fantastic project—the Unified Field Theory. But he died before he could complete it."

That small, pleasant reprieve following the disturbing events in Alpha Centauri ended in a sharp note from the computer. An alarm at Masters' controls lit red in concert with the klaxon. Masters read the warning and added his voice in counterpoint.

"Malfunction in computer guidance system. Switch to back up."

In response, Bowen vacated his seat at the chart table and took to the wall of instruments. There, he keyed in the proper code. The klaxon quieted and the warning lights cut out.

"Back up," Bowen called.

Altares performed another bank toward starboard. On the leveling off, a second alarm sounded. Masters saw the problem on visual before any of the instruments identified the threat.

"Meteor shower," he spat.

That slight course deviation put them in the path of dozens of objects. An inferno enveloped *Altares'* stem as her prow clipped the stellar debris field. Despite their speed, at first Masters was able to maneuver past the mass of the threat. Then another glancing blow impacted against the hull. *Altares* lurched upon contact—so violently that both pilots were nearly knocked from their seats. From the cut of his eye, Masters saw Anna tossed about. Mercifully, she snagged hold of a safety bar at the arch between compartments and held on for support.

One of the instrument panels directly above Masters' head erupted in a cascade of sparks. Other explosions crackled unseen from different sections of the Flight Deck and Navigation Area, the jolts accompanied by a shrieking alarm bell. The klaxon soon cut out, silenced by another of those explosions inside the ship.

An even more ominous warning replaced it. From the rear of the ship, past the Crew's Quarters and Monitoring Area, came the shrill whine of their main engine powering back up.

"The Photon Drive," Masters called above the noise. "It cut in. It just cut in!"

He stabbed at switches. None of Masters' efforts slowed the beast he piloted from charging.

"Tom?"

Bowen moved at the computer wall. Smoke poured from the controls. "Back up systems blown!"

One of the cluster's yellow stars appeared in their path, only this time it didn't look so small to Jane beyond the space window. The glowing mass quickly expanded, nearly blocking out all else on the map. They were going to collide, to plunge directly into that alien star's corona, where they'd burn up.

At her left, Jane saw her father wresting with the light ship's controls. *Altares* veered away from the doom she'd envisioned, the Flight Deck awash in blinding golden light as she passed farther on.

Bowen was now with them, his eyes wide and not blinking. David, too, rushed in from

Navigation.

"Guidance systems down," the boy reported.

Bowen barked, "Skipper, cut the drive!"

It was clear that Masters was struggling to accomplish just that. "Linkage jammed! Jane, activate the failsafe system."

Jane turned from the mad view of stars rushing past, each one ravenous to devour *Altares*, and stabbed at their final option. The failsafe screen activated, and instantly she sensed the Photon Drive cut out, telegraphed as weight lifted off her and the rush of stars floating past slowed.

Ahead of *Altares*, the view stabilized. A trio of golden stars burned on the far side of the space window.

Relief washed over Jane. She fidgeted in her chair, sucked down a deep breath, and turned to see a similar emotion on Anna's face. The joy proved short-lived.

The bright red telltale flickered, indicating the failsafe was engaged.

"Oh no," Jane said.

She thumbed the system again. The failsafe, like so many of their vital systems, puffed out caustic smoke. The red light wavered, warning of imminent failure. Soon.

"Failsafe not responding," Jane said. "It's blown!"

Jane boosted up from the copilot's chair and attempted to reroute the command through other instruments at her disposal. The failsafe cut out. *Altares* trembled as the Photon Drive again powered up.

Masters gripped the controls. "There's no way," he said. "I can't cut the drive!"

The unmistakable whine from the engines ramped up. They resumed accelerating. *Altares* arrowed forward, passing another yellow star and its binary mate, a red dwarf that filled the cockpit with searing rose-colored light.

"Then we're just going to keep on accelerating?" Bowen asked.

Anna sighed, "God help us."

A more scientific response came from the crew's youngest member, who held onto the back of the pilot's chair. "But we can't keep on accelerating. I mean, nothing can travel faster than light…can it, Dad?"

"That's what the theory says."

The whine from the Photon Drive intensified. With it, so did the pressure born of their quickening velocity.

Masters reached for his harness and buckled it. "Forget the theory—just strap yourselves in!"

Jane was already securing herself in the copilot's chair. The others hastened back into the Navigation Area. *Altares* tilted to port. Anna grabbed hold of the safety rail between compartments. A trinary cluster of yellow stars raced past the porthole.

Bowen and David made it safely into

their seats at the chart table. Anna scurried by, headed to the Monitoring Area. The ship banked again toward her port side. Anna made it to the next of the safety bars running in a line along walls.

"Are you all right?" Bowen called over his shoulder.

"Yes," Anna answered. "Yes, I'm fine."

Altares raced beyond the trinary stars. As the gravitational pull they exerted relaxed, the light ship leveled out. But her velocity increased — 99,000 miles per second and climbing. The force pressed against Anna. Her grip on the bar slipped.

Then the force carried her off her feet, through the Monitoring Area and Crew's Quarters, and slammed her into the Photon Drive's barrier doors.

Chapter Ten

Their training between spaceports and Delta Station should have brought them closer, Bowen thought. Bonding them again through the possibilities, the dangers and thrills of the *Altares* Mission alike. Only the frost building between them at Beta deepened. By the time of their arrival to Delta Station, it had formed a wall between husband and wife.

Bowen heard Anna cry out as the pressure inside the light ship flung her backward and then the collision when she struck the Photon Drive's partition. Whatever had caused that early chill to thicken into permafrost no longer mattered. Bowen imagined the wall of ice shattering as he turned, fighting the stress determined to pin him flat against his chair.

Anna was pressed to the transparent barrier, her feet off the floor, her mouth opened wide in an expression of silent pain.

"I'm coming over," Bowen called.

He threw off his safety harness and kicked up from the seat. The forces unleashed within *Altares* pushed against him. Standing felt more like climbing as muscles transformed to stone. He made it halfway out of his seat before the overwhelming weight slammed him back down.

"No," Anna answered. "No, Tom…no!"

Altares accelerated. More stars raced past, there one moment beyond the space windows, gone the next.

Masters noted the velocity gage had reached 170,000 miles per second, with no indication of slowing. He blinked, and their speed jumped up to 175,000.

And then he felt those sickening waves of distortion, attempting to rend flesh and muscle off bone. The pressure grabbed hold of his organs, seeming determined to do more than separate skin from skeleton—body from soul as well.

Anna remained pinned against the transparent wall. Bowen made another futile attempt to reach her. As he rose, he saw that David was unconscious.

"Anna?"

No response came. The pressure slammed Bowen back against his chair, and he slipped away.

A sound like thunder filled Masters' ears.

The velocity gage now read past 183,000 miles per second. The view of space beyond the direct vision window had renounced the recognizable masses of alien stars in ones, duos, and trinary groups. Now, everything was blurred together into a fast-moving cyclone of light through which *Altares* shot.

Jane had blacked out, he saw, after struggling a look over to the copilot's chair. Not far behind, Masters followed her into oblivion.

Altares raced onward.

Something about her surroundings seemed familiar.

"Jane," the woman whispered.

A chill gossiped over Jane's flesh as she moved through the darkness, feeling her way along a length of wall that had been scorched long ago, according to the skeins of cobweb draped between grooves and protrusions.

"Where are you going, girl?" the voice taunted more than asked. "You can't escape. The time for that has ended."

Jane continued through the shadowy landscape, aware of the roughness under her fingertips, the incongruity, the wall her only guide and anchor. The voice degenerated into a deep, raspy attempt at breath that seemed to be all around her, one with the darkness.

Her fingers slipped over something cool and flat. Jane dug in her treads. A window? The shape and slickness suggested one, at least. Jane pulled back her right hand into her uniform jacket and made a cloth of the sleeve. She wiped at the cold surface, cleaning away enough soot that the area surrounding her lightened noticeably. She scrubbed harder, but the glass was burned. Given its odd asymmetry, it was possible that she hadn't discovered a window at all but slag, some component of the landscape melted or fused during whatever cataclysm befell this place.

More breathing noises followed, the intake sounding as though air was being sucked in through a filter of wet cotton. Jane ceased wiping at the glass and peered out. A star map waited beyond the window, black velvet dotted by endless silver light points. She ducked down and angled for a better view. There, up above the vague outline of the dead planet—that *obscenity!*

The massive space station in the shape of a double helix drifted into view beyond Jane's prison, its image distorted by the warped glass. In the brief time Jane studied the monstrosity, the air around her cooled. Her insides tensed.

"Who are you?" Jane asked. Once the words were out, she clamped her teeth shut to keep them from chattering.

"Someone who needs you."

"You need our help? Were you the one who contacted us at Alpha Centauri?"

"Alpha Centauri," the voice spat. "How long ago that feels now, given time's hunger."

Jane choked down a heavy swallow and found that her mouth had gone completely dry from fear. "It was you!"

More labored breathing. With her eyes locked on the distorted vision of the colossus in orbit around a dead Earth, it struck Jane that the sound of respiration appeared to originate *from* the wall. She backed away from the window and into the surrounding shadows.

"Tell me who you are."

The walls exhaled. "An explorer of the universe, like you, dear Jane."

Jane spun around, performing a 360-degree turn. The darkness enveloped her like a shroud. She willed herself to wake up. A dream, that's all this was. A nightmare. The worst she'd ever suffered. But the dream remained intact.

"No," she sobbed.

The voice from the shadows answered with a malevolent laugh. "Don't you believe me? Believe that I have gone to places no one should dare to visit? That I have returned and, yes, the darkness followed?"

The floor cloaked in night beneath her soles took on the wall's incongruity. Jane backtracked and reached out. The cool surface of the space window tingled beneath her palm.

"This isn't real," she said, despite the evidence presented to senses.

"Isn't it?"

She reversed away from the window, feeling her way along the wall. The foul smell of singed circuitry intensified. With it was an element worse than the caustic odor of burnt tech. It was seared flesh, her inner voice declared, just as something fixed to that length of dark wall seized hold of her trembling hand. Jane screamed. Her voice resonated through the darkness, and echoed back at her, amplified tenfold.

"Oh yes, Jane," the voice said in counterpoint from every direction. "I need you!"

She tugged against the misshapen hand jutting out from the scorched metal wall. Even in her panic, she gleaned it wasn't human—the fingers wrapped around hers more like tentacles than digits. Jane pulled free. Part of the alien hand came with her, severed from the rest of its anatomy yet still clutching at her. The lump of flesh disintegrated into ashes as she struggled to shake it off, the texture reminding her of dead leaves in autumn.

The shadows ahead of her brightened. Unimaginable alien technology powered up, and the stagnant air thrummed with an undercurrent of building energy. Movement teased Jane's eyes. She faced the disturbance. The darkness shook. A sound her imagination translated into fingernails scrabbling along the walls tore through the frigid air, from what could only be numerous hands.

The hands reached toward her. Jane screamed again. In that last instant, she saw the source of the voice and of her nightmare: an inhuman mass suspended from the ceiling by lengths of bioluminescent web.

No, Jane realized in a moment of clarity during which she was able to view the creature with more curiosity than fear or revulsion—it was connected to its surroundings by cables and power conduits, the source of the faint glow.

It grabbed her with its multitude of alien talons.

Jane jolted awake, barely managing to trap another scream before it powered up her throat.

"Jane," a different voice called. "Jane!"

It belonged to her father.

Altares sat idling, her mad dash across the galactic core ended. A bloated red giant star floated beyond the space window, its rose-colored light bathing the Flight Deck. Jane's heart continued to hammer inside her chest. She was convinced that if she closed her eyes again, she'd return to that horrific place.

"Dad?" She shifted in the copilot's chair and came fully back from the abyss.

"Hi," Masters said.

"The Photon Drive?"

Masters exhaled. "Yeah, Jane. The failsafe cut back in and put the Drive into reverse thrust."

Jane looked up at the instruments. True to her father's claim, the telltale was lit red and showed no sign of wavering.

Behind them, Bowen stirred. He reached

for David. The boy woke.

"Are you all right?"

David nodded. "Yes. How's Mother?"

Bowen turned. Anna's body was sprawled across the section of floor in front of the transparent safety partitions leading to the Photon Drive. He unhooked his harness and scrambled over on shaky legs. To his relief, when he was halfway across the Monitoring Area, Anna recovered. Bowen hurried the rest of the way and helped her to stand.

"Easy," he said. "Easy, sweetheart."

Anna leaned against him. "I'm all right."

Bowen's grip tightened. For a wonderful moment, she rested her head against his and smiled when their eyes connected. But then she stiffened.

"The children?"

"They're fine," Bowen said.

They walked together into the Navigation Area. David joined them, and Anna pulled him into her arms.

The sound of buttons being repeatedly stabbed and tested filtered back from the Flight Deck.

"No power at all now," they heard Masters say. "That wild acceleration must have burnt out some of the Drive units."

"I wonder where we are," Jane added.

Bowen turned from Anna and David toward the porthole, and its view of the massive red star beyond the light ship's starboard wing.

"Where indeed," he sighed.

Chapter Eleven

Without her Photon Drive, *Altares* might as well have been dead where she sat. The ship's generator kept lights powered and maintained heat—and the atmosphere filters had removed the bitter edge of burned circuitry from the air, there was that much to be grateful for. But the ship would only get so far on her sub-light chemical drive and steering rockets.

The red giant star holding off their starboard reminded Masters of a vast, bloodshot unblinking eye, constantly watching them. At least the Drive had cut out far enough away to spare them from waking up deeper inside its gravisphere. Or worse—on a collision course, or so close to its corona that they burned up.

He gave the controls one last try. Still dead, as expected. Sighing in frustration, Masters vacated the pilot's chair and crossed into Navigation. All three of the Bowen family were checking instruments—Anna for damages to the ship's systems, he assumed, while Bowen and David worked to get a fix on their present location.

"What have we got?" Masters asked.

David answered, "Space and time coordinates gone, Captain."

Masters' frustration grew. "Gone? That's great. So we've no idea how long we were unconscious, nor how far we've traveled."

Anna offered the sole bright spot to the report. "At least all of our life support systems are working."

"Well, that's something. But they won't help us find out where we are." He turned to Bowen. "Tom, can you get a fix on our position? We've got to know how far off course we are."

He could tell by the grim expression on the other man's face that the answer wouldn't be good. "No can do, Skipper. The computer can't recognize any of the stars out there."

Bowen's words ironed all the emotion off Masters' face. "That's impossible. It would mean that we're off course by billions of miles."

Bowen's throat knotted under the influence of a heavy swallow. "That's right."

"What about Space Beacon Delta?" David offered. "Couldn't we get a fix on that?"

"How about it, Tom?" Masters pressed.

"We could try, but finding that beacon, well, it's like hunting for a needle in a billion haystacks," Bowen said. "You've got to face it, Skipper—we're lost."

Masters turned away. He sat on the corner of the chart table, the defeat in his body language impossible to misread. "Yeah, and we're going to stay lost without that Photon Drive. Anna, what's the heat level inside the Chamber?"

Anna said, "It's way up, but I'll check it. The Drive's shut down, so there's no radiation hazard."

She crossed into the Monitoring Area. Both Masters and Jane followed.

Anna tapped out a sequence on the Chamber's instrument panel. One monitor rewarded her with a printout. She scanned the report and then handed it to Masters for review.

"Heat insulation's weakened," she said. "It's like a furnace in there."

"Okay, we wait until it cools."

Bowen chimed in from the Navigation Area. "I wouldn't wait too long, Skipper."

Masters saw that the other man held a clipboard upon which the latest data relating to their position in space was gathered.

"*Altares* is caught in the gravitational pull of that sun out there."

The red giant looming beyond the portholes appeared closer, Masters agreed, its glow brighter. In the seconds that followed Bowen's declaration, he swore he felt the ship drifting, the star hungry for *Altares* and her crew.

That sealed it.

"Right, we go in now," Masters said.

"In that heat?" Anna countered. "How long do you think you could survive in there?"

"You tell me."

Anna considered the question. "Well, if you wear the heat suit, about fifteen minutes. No more."

"Then we do it in relays. I'll go in first," Masters said. He eyed the nearest direct vision port and the red glare pouring through. "Tom, you and Anna get all the dope you can on our rate of drift."

"Right, Skipper," Bowen said.

Masters started back in the direction of the Crew's Quarters. "Jane, help me on with the suit," he called over his shoulder.

Anna stopped him in place. "Harry, I mean it — fifteen minutes maximum."

As Masters and Jane continued on, and David resumed his attempt to pick up Delta Station's beacon, *Altares'* drift quickened, the light ship pulled toward the red giant.

Anna checked her figures. She set the clock at a fifteen-minute countdown. Even one minute in that heat was dangerous. Anything beyond fifteen, a death sentence.

Masters fastened the neck of the silver heat-resistant suit. Jane helped him on with the gloves. He caught the girl staring past him and toward the big metal door leading into the

Photon Drive Chamber.

"You will be careful in there, won't you, Dad?" Jane said. "No risks."

Masters forced a smile. "Sure, I'll be careful."

"We don't want to lose our captain, do we? Let alone my father."

Masters set both gloved hands on the sides of Jane's face, leaned down, and kissed her forehead, his only answer before reaching for the suit's protective helmet. "Well, here we go."

He donned the helmet. Jane helped to secure the bib and nape fasteners. That accomplished, she signaled that he was set by a pat to the shoulder. Masters approached the Photon Drive Chamber.

Anna released the inner door. The Chamber's protective seal swung open, revealing the white-hot glare from inside. As Masters plodded toward the Chamber's maw, toolkit in hand, the suit, already tight against his physique, seemed to constrict even more. And then he remembered.

After their mad race across the star map.

After succumbing to the stress of those forces attempting to rip skin from muscle, muscle from bone, bone from soul.

After.

For a time, his unconscious soul had traveled to someplace *other*. It was dark there, a realm of shadows nearly devoid of all light. The agony he'd suffered behind *Altares'* pilot controls was nothing compared to this new misery. The pain here was exquisite and knew no end.

A land of eternal pain, and with it came terror to match. Masters was blind and yet he somehow saw; dead, and also alive.

Masters stopped in place. The open Chamber glowed before him. What he'd experienced after blacking out was only a dream, nothing more. What he now faced was real. The time afforded him was little enough to begin with, and already being squandered on memories from a nightmare. He shook off his paralysis and willed the dream to vanish. Masters' body resisted fully waking up. He privately cursed the loss of those seconds and entered the Chamber.

The heavy door swung shut behind him.

Space inside was tight, and the chill he suffered at remembering the horrific dream vanished, driven out by temperatures that reached him through the suit's protection. Masters walked with caution along the tubular Main Photon Drive manifold conduit, the mechanism connecting all parts of the light ship from particle scoop through flight controls and main engine.

He maneuvered along the manifold and reached the first of his targets. Heat had swollen the Linkage door, and it took all of his strength to force open the panel. Once that was accomplished, he switched off the damaged relays and opened all of the intact backup units. That accomplished, he rolled the door back into position before turning his attention to the Drive itself.

A red sign on that section of the manifold warned: DANGER—DRIVE UNITS. Masters scanned the first and second of the units. Both were functioning, if not able to activate. The third unit sent the scanner from his toolkit into a panic. He'd located the source of their problem.

One minute down.

Masters reached for the safety cover. The metal had started to distort in the heat. He redoubled his effort and the lid released. With its surrender, the damaged Drive unit launched a plume of superheated air and vapor up from the manifold, along with a blinding release of photonic glare. It was as if, Masters thought, he was staring into the corona of a miniature sun. The analogy wasn't far off point; the fuel that allowed them to travel at such fantastic speeds threw off a searing blast. A small star, one of several chambered inside the Photon Drive.

Altares pitched toward her starboard. Masters adjusted position to stop himself from tripping—*falling*—into the tiny star in the damaged Drive unit and being burned alive in spite of his protective gear.

The light ship was accelerating, he knew, toward a similar death in the corona of the red giant pulling them nearer, nearer, with every merciless tick of the clock.

Chapter Twelve

Jane kept *Altares* level using short bursts from the steering rockets. As the red giant's drag intensified, the likelihood of the ship going into a roll increased. Once that happened, they'd spiral out of control, and none of the repairs her father hoped to accomplish would matter.

The others worked behind her — Bowen at the wall of instruments, David at the chart table. Anna, she saw through a quick glance over her shoulder, paced outside the Chamber partition.

A high-pitched note crackled over the intercom. The blast cut out as soon as it was picked up. It wasn't Delta Station's beacon.

Nine minutes.

Anna ceased pacing and entered the Navigation Area. "Tom, what have you got?"

"Our rate of drift is steadily increasing," he answered. "But we're a long way from the point of no return. Still, I'll feel better once our skipper finishes making those repairs. How about you?"

The distant look was back on Anna's face. Bowen lowered his clipboard and set his free hand on her shoulder. Anna allowed the connection—a good sign, he thought, even if her news wasn't.

"Well, I've been taking some readings on the red sun. They're not adding up."

Bowen eyed Anna's clipboard. "Let's see."

Not lost on him was their physical closeness. Whatever the source of Anna's worry, he wasn't involved.

"Comparing it to our own Earth sun, its radius is ten thousand times larger, its mass is only twice as large, and its density—now this is the incredible thing—its density is less than a millionth of our own. I don't like it."

Bowen considered her findings and shared the concern written on his wife's face.

"What do you think?" she asked.

Bowen said, "It's unstable, that's for sure. Dangerous, even. Anna, these figures..."

"Yes?"

"They speak for themselves: increased surface temperature, abnormal expansion rate. That sun out there has just about had it."

The intercom chirped. Bowen broke away from the conversation and answered.

"Skipper?"

Inside the Chamber, Masters struggled to remove the damaged Drive unit. "Tom, I've fixed the Linkage system. The insulation has overheated. That was no trouble at all, but one of the Photon Drive units is completely burned out."

"Can you replace it?"

Jane vacated the copilot's chair and took in the conversation from the arch between compartments.

"Yeah, if I can get it out," Masters answered, his voice strained. "It's fused in solid."

Bowen acknowledged the update with a nod. "How long?"

"Well, I'm not going to hang about, that's for sure."

Bowen imagined their captain struggling to unlock the unit from the manifold, the working space tight, the heat volcanic.

"But if I can't get it fixed in time, Tom, you'll have to take over."

"All right, Skipper," Bowen said. The conversation ended, he faced the chart table. "David, leave that and check our rate of drift."

The boy carried out his order.

"Anna, we'd better set up a full sensor analysis on that sun right away."

Anna returned to the Monitoring Area. Jane crossed from the arch to the nearest porthole. The red mass off their starboard wing seethed at more than twice the size it had been when they'd awakened in the system. It could have been the gravitational drag or something far worse alluded to in Bowen's discussion with Anna.

Altares drifted closer.

Jane glanced down through the porthole to see the light ship's superstructure glowing red.

The girl approached Anna in the Monitoring Area.

"It's a red giant, isn't it? A dying star."

Anna looked up from the scanning instruments. "Looks like it."

"That means it could explode at any minute."

"Or next month, or next year," Anna said. She faced Jane. "It is unstable, but it could stay as it is for a hundred years."

Jane shot a look at the clock. Twelve minutes had elapsed. "It's taking him a long time, isn't it?" Before Anna could respond, Jane added, "Did you feel it, too? After we accelerated and lost consciousness?"

Anna shrugged. "It?"

"The dark place, where everything's burned up."

"Jane?" Anna asked.

But then she remembered the nightmare in which she was suffocating in the shadows, and in more pain than she'd ever experienced. The vision receded, but the shock remained palpable in the mad beating of her heart and the sudden chill atop her skin.

Masters pulled. Finally, the damaged unit separated from the manifold. With it came more plumes of superheated air and a blinding effulgence of photons. *Almost there*, he thought.

The heat verged on unbearable. An image attempted to form in his mind's eye, that of the suit collapsing, his insides—bones included—liquefied. He drove the picture out. Then Masters' inner voice told him it was better to melt than burn.

He returned to the dream's darkness. Masters' next breath came with difficulty.

"No," he growled out loud, and readied to finish the repairs in the last sparse minutes remaining.

One of the alarms near Anna's sensors activated, drawing their attention through a loud, sharp warning. Anna hurried over to the spectrometer keeping watch on the red giant. A glance into the scope confirmed what the klaxon already knew. The surface of their greedy new neighbor in space seethed with instability.

Anna moved over to another instrument studying the red giant. "Tom," she called into Navigation.

Bowen and David joined her in the Monitoring Area.

"What is it?" Bowen asked.

"Massive neutrino emissions from the red sun."

Bowen leaned down for a look into the scope. "That's it. It's going to be a supernova."

"*Supernova*," David said. "That's just about the most colossal explosion that ever was!"

The alarm continued its wail. The accompanying warning light flashed red, mirroring the sun outside *Altares'* space windows and the reasons behind its agitated flashing.

"We've got to tell the captain," said Anna.

Behind them, Jane shouted, "No!"

They turned.

"If you tell him, he'll stay in there. He'll take the risks," Jane said.

"Jane, we're all at risk," said Anna.

Bowen returned to the intercom. "Skipper…"

Masters acknowledged, "Yeah?"

"Okay, listen! We've got to get the ship away from here. That red sun is about to go supernova."

Masters continued his repair work, the stress audible in his voice. "How much time?"

"Minutes, Skipper. Just minutes. Can you do it?"

Masters said he could.

Bowen switched off the intercom.

Jane raced over to where the trio stood, her panic no longer contained. "But he's got to come out!"

"He's got to fix the Photon Drive, Jane," said Anna.

David offered, "Couldn't we use the rocket motors—use our secondary engines to get us out of the system?"

"They haven't the power nor the speed," said Bowen. "They'd never pull us clear in time."

Jane again faced the clock. Thirteen minutes. Her father had nearly run out of time.

Masters remembered the house on Rankine Lane. It was long before *Altares*. He was fixing something, maybe the solar-based heating system that warmed the cottage's water supply. Whatever the repair job, the thing rewarded him with a painful jolt that traveled up his wrist before disbursing harmlessly. A simple, sharp warning, so long ago that he couldn't remember how he'd earned it. But the body never truly forgot, and the sting pulsed again all these years later, shocking him out of the past.

He realized he'd locked up and was barely still standing, almost slumped over the Photon Drive's manifold. Shaking fully out of the daze, he cursed whatever time had been lost and refocused. The Drive unit—if he didn't complete the repair, the giant red eye drawing *Altares* into its unwanted embrace would finally blink. And then…

Masters resumed. Rankine Lane was a

good place, and he'd been happy there with Jane and her mother. So much so, that when Sylvia died, the only chance at being happy again had been to go as far away from that place and all they'd lost there as was possible.

They'd traveled so far that even the computers didn't recognize the stars.

And one of those stars was about to devour them.

He worked the replacement Drive unit into position and secured it. Then, Masters slid down to the base of the manifold. A few more connections and he'd be done—only he worried the seconds wouldn't be there, and that time had run out.

Chapter Thirteen

Some of the readings were perplexing. David chuckled to himself at the notion. Perplexing? Their rate of drift into the dying red giant's clutches had nearly doubled over the course of the past minute. Momentum built. So did the threat of being caught in the monstrous blast wave when that nearby sun gave up the ghost and went supernova.

No, the intelligence he found as curious as it was disturbing came from a different set of reports related to their present crisis with the Photon Drive. To pass the long minutes, he'd run a systems-wide diagnostic. More than *Altares'* Photon Drive had been damaged during the light ship's mad charge through unexplored space. They needed to know how extensive that damage was, and so he'd operated the program in the background while their captain labored to fix the Drive and David sought Delta Station's elusive long-range beacon.

The boy moved to the nearest porthole. Space outside that window blazed a fiery red. At their present range, he didn't need the Monitoring Area's spectrometer to gage the changes taking place across the dying star. The collapse wove vast shadows through the blood-colored haze.

The information sent back from the particle scoop would have to wait until *Altares* was free of the red giant's gravitational pull. *If...*

Jane stood in front of the Drive partition, her eyes locked on the sealed door. She turned toward David, her expression mirroring his.

The red giant seethed.

Altares continued to fall.

The clock counted down.

Fourteen minutes had elapsed.

Jane broke away from her position standing guard in front of the partition and activated the radio. "Dad...*dad*, you must come out!"

Masters answered, "Take it easy, honey—we're almost there."

Anna guided Jane over to the nearest chair and coaxed her down. "Jane, when we were in training—"

"I know, they told us of the dangers," the girl said, barely controlling her tears. "I just didn't think it could happen. Not to us."

"It hasn't yet."

Jane wiped at her eyes and composed herself. "I'm all right."

David watched their exchange, distracted from the knowledge he had yet to share with the rest of the crew. The particle scoop—if the analysis proved correct, it could explain everything, including the Photon Drive's erratic behavior. The burden of his suspicions welled inside him like a malady. He thought about telling his mother and Jane. Another look out the porthole convinced him that the knowledge would have to wait, and the burden worsened, helped along by the image of the red sun, now ejecting prominences a million miles past its corona.

Masters worked to connect the new Drive unit replacement.

Bowen stopped pacing long enough for another glimpse into the spectrometer. The sun's impending death neared, according to the massive streamers of flame blasting forth from its surface. He straightened and cast a worried look at Anna.

The clock tolled in warning with an ominous screech. They had reached the fifteenth minute.

Jane exploded out of the chair. Anna caught her as she raced toward the Drive Chamber door.

Bowen thumbed the intercom. "Harry,

come on out. I'll take over."

"I'm nearly finished."

Bowen said, "Skipper, you're beyond the limit!"

Masters continued the arduous task of securing the replacement unit, his laugh lost to the hiss of superheated vapor. "You think I don't know that?"

The warning's shriek played without interruption. The dying star's casting off of its energy spread, with the first ejection of mass from its surface.

Altares shook.

David turned away from the porthole. "It's happening!"

Bowen reached for the extra set of heat-insulated gloves. Without the rest of the suit's protection, he wouldn't last a full minute inside the Photon Drive Chamber.. Not that they had the luxury of that much time.

"You'd better get in your positions," he barked above the constant shriek of alarm bells.

At first, no one moved, all the crew's attention trained upon the Photon Drive Chamber.

Masters struggled back in the direction of the Linkage panel. He was well past the maximum point allotted to him inside the Chamber, but was still on his feet. He wondered if he was dead, only his body wasn't yet aware that it had expired, burned up inside the heat suit. He even laughed out loud at the notion. The rawness in his throat was a solid reminder that he was alive.

Reaching for the control panel, he guessed as to why. At just after the fifteen-minute mark, he'd made the final corrections, and the system that cooled the fantastic heat inside the Chamber switched on. The temperature around him had easily been cut in half.

Masters thumbed all of the functioning links back online. The panel lit ACTIVE. One problem solved, a very big one. But an even larger danger loomed in its wake, according to the chatter from the crew.

He hit the door release. The massive protective panel trundled open. Masters stepped out. Through the helmet's fogged-over visor, he saw Jane charge toward him.

"Dad!" she cried.

Bowen caught her. "No, Jane—stay behind the partition!"

The other man helped Masters off with his helmet and through the barrier, into the Monitoring Area. He eased Masters down onto the nearest sleep couch. Again, the girl made a reach for her father. Bowen deflected her away for a second time.

"Don't, Jane. His suit's too hot!"

Masters wiggled free of the suit's top. "I fixed it, Tom. I fixed it."

"We've got to get this ship out of here,"

Bowen said. "Jane, get going."

Jane nodded but lingered as Anna opened a cabinet containing medical supplies. The ship's doctor grabbed in intravenous pen and was about to inject Masters' arm when Bowen noticed their copilot still hovering beside the couch.

"Jane, I said go! Get this ship moving," Bowen said. "Anna, go with her."

Jane hurried through to the Flight Deck. Anna followed.

"You all right, Skipper?" Bowen asked.

Masters nodded. "Yeah," he said as David strapped him into the couch's harness.

Jane took to the pilot's chair, Anna the copilot's. Both buckled in. Behind them in Navigation, Bowen and David did the same.

Jane skipped the checklist—there wasn't time. She powered up the Photon Drive. "Full acceleration," she called above the telltale, building whine.

Searing prominences lashed outward from the red giant. *Altares* fought against the star's grip and pulled free. The light ship shot away at faster and faster speeds. Within seconds, they'd put an additional half-million miles between them and the star. But that was hardly enough.

Altares' velocity quickened.

At the light ship's back, the red giant came apart in an effulgence of blinding white energy. The massive explosion soon caught up, knocking *Altares* off her axis and straight trajectory. The light ship spiraled. Jane fought against the roll before it shook them apart and aimed their nose back on course.

The Photon Drive held, keeping *Altares* barely ahead of the destruction clawing at her aft.

The view was spectacular, now that they were far enough from the supernova's ravages. Space had been transformed into a kaleidoscope. Each second widened the distance between *Altares* and the vibrant remains of the red sun. Before long, the breathtaking vision was lost to the void.

Every object that had been loose upon their mad dash away from the red giant now littered the floor, from the Flight Deck through Navigation. Holdalls had spilled their contents across the Crew's Quarters. Some instruments lay smashed in the Monitoring Area. But the light ship was intact, her crew alive, all buckled safely to seats.

"I think we made it," Jane said to Anna.

Masters released his harness and stood. Anna vacated the copilot's chair and intercepted him at the arch to Navigation.

"Easy now," she admonished. "Where do you think you're going? Come on, sit down."

She helped him over to a seat and clipped medical electrodes to his uniform shirt. The bio-telemetry panel activated, displaying the captain's vital signs along with the three-dimensional cut away of his circulatory and respiration systems.

"How do you feel?"

Masters struggled down a breath. "Never better. How are we doing?"

Anna ran an eye over the panel's findings. Everything looked good. "No damage. And we're clear of that exploding star."

"Thank God," Masters said. "Where's Jane?"

"Piloting the ship," Anna said.

Masters smiled.

"You should have seen her. Cool as you like. Cool as her father in the pilot's chair."

Masters chuckled. "Yeah, well don't tell her that. She already suffers from a lack of modesty."

Anna unclipped the electrodes. The bio-telemetry panel dimmed. "You took a double beating. My advice is to rest up."

She didn't expect him to listen, and Masters didn't disappoint. "Remind me to do that some time."

He marched into the Flight Deck. Jane switched over to automatic before vacating her seat and meeting his hug.

"Good girl," Masters said.

"Dad," she sighed. "Dad, I was so frightened."

Masters held Jane close. The sound of

footsteps, soft across the floor, drove them apart. David had entered from the Navigation Area.

"Captain," the boy said, his formal tone matching the tense look on his face. "There's something you should see."

Chapter Fourteen

Altares floated at standstill in the dark emptiness between star systems.

The crew gathered in the Navigation Area around the chart table, where David sat.

"Before we escaped the red giant," he explained, "I ran a ship-wide scanning program in order to see what else had been damaged by the malfunction in the Photon Drive."

"And?" Masters asked.

"Nothing that can't be repaired, now that we're clear of the supernova, Captain," David said. "But while diagnosing the engine systems, I found something that explains why the Drive went haywire."

He punched a button on the controls. The chart table's screen switched from the real time feed being broadcast of the surrounding star map to a diagram of *Altares*. The picture focused on the ship's particle scoop apparatus. An indicator light flashed, directing the eye to the scoop filters set inside their tube muzzles.

"The primary function of the scoop is to collect photons from space, which we then use to power the Drive," David said. "The Drive stores them in three units and then releases them at an accelerated speed, taking us along for the ride."

Bowen narrowed his eyes. "What does the scoop have to do with the Drive malfunction?"

David thumbed another button. A second window pulled down. It displayed a blurred image of something that glowed white-hot, like a photon, only much more intense.

"The filters are set to differentiate photons from other energy sources. Somehow, we took on this," David said.

"What is it?" asked Jane.

"It isn't photonic," David said. "My best guess and the computer's is that it's superluminal."

The answer elicited shock from his captive audience.

"*Super*luminal." This came from Masters.

David nodded. "Yes, a particle capable of traveling faster than the speed of light. A tachyon, maybe. Whatever it is got committed into the engine manifold soon after our launch from Delta Station and has been jumping around inside the system. According to the damage report, it's what blew out the Drive unit and caused the massive power up."

Anna leaned down for a better look at the indistinct micro-star that had fueled their ship and sent it hurtling at unimaginable speed. "A superluminal. Are you—or the computer—suggesting that we may have traveled at faster than light velocity?"

"Yes," Masters said. "I didn't believe it, figured it was a trick on my eyes. And with all the stress of flying at that rate..."

A heavy silence descended over the crew. From the periphery, Masters saw Jane fidget in place, her eyes refusing to meet anyone else's. She appeared to be in need of furthering the discussion. He was about to nudge her when her trembling lips parted, and she spoke.

"There's more," Jane said. "Haven't you all felt it?"

More silence followed, then David said, "The dark room."

"Yes," Jane said, looking so relieved by David's confession that Masters thought she might cry. "Only it wasn't just a room. I was there. That place was in orbit around the Earth."

"Earth?" Anna parroted.

Jane nodded. "But the planet was dead, and there was a giant space station in orbit, one bigger than Delta and the new Epsilon combined."

"I don't remember that," Masters said.

Jane met her father's gaze. "But-?"

"It was different for me," Masters said. "I

couldn't breathe. I was—"

"Suffocating," Bowen interrupted. "And it was the worst pain conceivable. The kind that, by all rights, causes a man to black out. Only there wasn't any escape from it."

"Not ever," Anna said.

No one spoke after that for what seemed a long sum of time. Only *Altares* broke the pall, in the background hum of repaired engine systems and the melody of her computers.

"There's someone aboard that place," Jane said, her voice barely louder than a whisper. "An old woman. Only she isn't human. It was she that contacted us in Alpha Centauri. She stole the scroll satellite."

"How do you know?" asked Masters.

"She spoke to me. There's something she wants from us."

"What is it?" Masters asked.

Jane shrugged. She hadn't realized she'd dipped her right hand into her pocket and was rolling Winnie's snowflake dog tag through her fingers like a charm or amulet until the cold metal against her skin triggered a shiver.

Masters straightened. "David, continue to scan for the Delta Beacon. Anna, I'd like the ship's eyes—and her laser scopes—to be on the lookout for anything anomalous. And I'd like them to warn us before anything gets too close."

Anna nodded. "Any suggestions on what that anomaly will look like?"

"A nightmare," Masters said.

Repairs continued, mostly in silence, the melody of the sensor sweep around *Altares'* present position a constant reminder of the malevolence they all felt.

Masters listened again to the brief audio file.

"*Croatoan,*" the alien voice said. On the screen, the video of the dark mass floated against the red backdrop of Proxima Centauri, indistinct, like a thing not really there.

"That word," Jane said. "If it is a word…it sounds so familiar."

Anna crossed in from Navigation. "It very well could be. I ran it through the computer. Old Earth history — America in 1590. When John White returned from England to the Roanoke Colony, he found that all the colonists were missing without a trace except for a single clue: one word, etched into a post. The word 'croatoan'."

Guidance and propulsion checked out. All steering rockets, too. While Jane worked the instrument board, Masters checked the Directional Antenna, which housed one of the light ship's two defensive laser batteries. Those weapons had been designed for different opponents — asteroids and space debris that posed a collision threat to *Altares*. If there was some malevolent presence stalking them even this deep into the uncharted wilderness of the galaxy's core, he was happy to have the firepower at their disposal.

From the cut of his eye, he saw Jane had stopped working and was at the mercy of her private thoughts. He spoke her name. Jane looked up.

"What is it?" Masters asked.

"Did I make the right choice? Back at Alpha Centauri...if I'd said no about going farther out, we'd be on our way home and not lost."

Masters crossed the area of deck that separated them and took Jane in his arms. "I don't regret the decision."

Jane hugged back. "You don't?"

"No. Even with what's happened, how many of the people we knew back on Earth got front row seats to a red giant going supernova?"

Jane laughed. Good, he'd lightened her mood.

"This has been the best adventure," he continued. "I'm sure your mother would be proud."

Jane's grip tightened. "I miss her so much."

"Yeah, me, too."

They held each other. Then Bowen's excited voice called from the Navigation Area.

"Skipper! A signal! We're picking up a signal!"

They crowded around the radio receiver. At the moment, the only sounds crackling out were static. Then, a faint mechanical song looped across the background.

"It could be just a pulsar," David said. He narrowed the receiver. The melody intensified. "No, it's the Delta beacon!"

Bowen patted the boy's shoulder. "Quick, David—feed it into the computer before we lose it."

David bounded over to the nearest terminal and routed the signal through the main computer. That accomplished, Bowen printed out a hardcopy of the evidence.

"Confirmed," he said in an excited voice. "It *is* Delta!"

He and Masters shook hands. Anna joined the celebration.

"David," Bowen said. "Compute data code."

David calculated. Bowen printed off the results.

"That signal was transmitted fifteen years after we left Earth," the navigator reported.

"Really?" Jane asked. "*The Earth.*"

"That's right," Bowen continued. He faced Masters. "Skipper, that means we can now work out our position relative to Earth."

"It's the first real break we've had, Tom."

Masters reached out and gripped Bowen's upper arms.

"Give us our course, Tom. We're going home."

Masters hastened into the Flight Deck,

and Jane followed. The celebratory atmosphere didn't maintain for long. Bowen noticed Anna had moved to the Navigation Area's porthole. He recognized her expression—more proof of his wife's sadness.

"Anna," he said, taking his seat before the chart table. When she didn't respond, he spoke louder. "Doctor Bowen, I said we're on our way."

She turned toward him and offered an unconvincing smile.

Bowen again stood and joined her at the direct vision window with its view of their dark surroundings.

"What is it, sweetheart?" he asked.

"Fifteen years, Tom," she said. "My parents, your father...they'll be old, even dead by now."

"Anna, we're going home."

"Yes, Tom, we're going home."

She smiled again, but it was that same sad look. Anna attempted to move past him, in the direction of the Monitoring Area. Bowen stopped her.

"Anna, tell me," he said. "The truth."

She took his hand.

And then Anna confessed everything.

Chapter Fifteen

Chemical-fueled engines fired. Steering rockets put *Altares* into a graceful ninety-degree turn. The light ship faced the direction of home and engaged her Photon Drive.

"Course steady at nine point six degrees," Jane said.

Masters glanced up at their present heading. "Nine point six degrees? Are you sure?"

Jane looked up, too. The discrepancy was spelled out on the screen. "Well, that's not what I set it at."

Bowen's voice joined in from Navigation. "Skipper, we're off course. Alter to four point two."

Their navigator checked his screen, a scowl forming on his face. The conversation with Anna was still too fresh, the revelation beyond painful to digest. Controller Forbes. Then he recalled what he'd said to her, and how his little joke had made them both laugh, made it possible to continue together, aboard *Altares*.

"You and Forbes, that was a long time ago."

It *was*, Bowen supposed. After all, Anna had, in the final reckoning, chosen him over Forbes. She'd traveled to Alpha Centauri and far beyond rather than remain behind on Delta Station with the Controller. How much of her decision owed to David as opposed to their marriage was irrelevant; she'd sided with them, and so he was able to forgive her.

"There's no reason to speak more of this," Bowen had said in those minutes before correcting course toward Earth—minutes and long miles already falling behind them. And so he figured he didn't need to think more about it, either. He loved Anna. She loved him. They were aimed in the direction of home. Second chances and new beginnings.

Bowen blinked. The information spelled out on the chart table's screen was disturbing in its present form, and growing worse as *Altares* charged onward.

"Hold it, Skipper," he called. "We're coming under intense gravitational pull."

"Check and confirm course," Masters ordered.

Bowen tapped keys. The information appeared on the chart table's screen.

"Skipper, bear three degrees starboard and increase power."

Masters made the correction. *Altares* tilted, trembled. The gravity source had latched on and wasn't willing to let go.

"We're still held in the grip of whatever's out there," said Masters.

Bowen yelled, "More power!"

Masters fed the engines. The telltale whine from the Photon Drive upped its tempo in response.

He checked power readings and gripped the controls tighter. "Can't break it."

Bowen rushed from his seat to the computer, where a printout was already waiting. Anna joined him at the wall of instruments as he scanned the information.

"Tom, what is it?"

He set a hand on her shoulder. "Anna, activate the forward laser beam to these coordinates."

Bowen handed Anna the printout and hurried back to David's side at the chart table. Anna powered up the light ship's forward laser. The cannon extended forth from the Directional Antenna and locked onto that patch of seemingly empty space. Anna fired.

Altares shook as the streamer of electric-blue energy powerful enough to shatter meteorites and cleave comets or asteroids out of their path rocketed forth. The beam continued ahead for several miles on a straight course before bending, warping, out of its focused alignment and vanishing from the star map.

Eyes wide, Bowen observed. On his way into the Flight Deck, he passed Anna, the shock on his face impossible to misread.

"It's a black hole," he sighed.

Altares quivered around and beneath him. This got Bowen moving faster. He dashed into the cockpit.

"Captain, it's a singularity—we're being pulled toward the event horizon of a black hole!"

Masters absorbed the information. "Set tangential course bearing five degrees starboard."

Jane punched in the correction while Masters fought with the controls. *Altares* rocked on her axis. The Photon Drive glowed white hot, but the light ship's speed continued to decelerate. They were trapped in a powerful undertow, and being dragged backward toward the singularity's ravenous maw.

Altares' speed dropped to a crawl. Then, she began to fall back in the direction of the black hole.

"Are we holding?" Masters shouted above the Photon Drive's building cacophony.

Bowen answered. "Maybe…just maybe."

Masters half-turned around. "Anna, compute its mass. Find out what you can about it."

Anna raced from Navigation into the Monitoring Area.

"Tom, lock onto Delta Beacon and transmit the location of the black hole," Masters continued.

"Right," said Bowen.

"It won't help us, but maybe those who follow us."

Bowen homed onto the melody broadcast from Delta Station's beacon and relayed the report. David approached.

"Have we a chance, Dad?"

Bowen shrugged. "No one knows much about black holes, except that they are stars which have collapsed in on themselves. They not only bend light but can actually swallow it."

The report was off. As he and David marched into the Flight Deck, Bowen sensed the quiver in the floor underfoot. They were falling in reverse despite the Photon Drive's output, being dragged stern first toward the black hole's event horizon.

Anna joined the rest of the crew around the pilot's and copilot's chairs in time to hear the latest update from *Altares'* captain.

"It's no good," said Masters. "We can't break free."

He gunned the Photon Drive up to maximum. The most it did was slow their fall, delay the inevitable. With engines taxed and complaining of the stress put upon them, *Altares* soon resumed her backward slide.

And then the light ship jolted to a complete stop.

Jane turned toward Masters. "Dad?"

Masters checked the instruments. Their momentum had halted. "Course frozen. We're not losing any more ground!"

"But how?" asked Bowen.

Jane felt the answer in the chill suddenly creeping over her flesh, seconds before the proximity alarm warned of another near-space object moving on an approach vector toward *Altares*.

Masters activated the screen. But from the cut of her eye, Jane caught the slither of movement through the space window as something out there drifted between the light ship and the stars, cutting off their glow.

"Powered object," Masters said. "They've got us in some kind of magnetic beam."

"It's our alien friends," David said. "The ones from Alpha Centauri."

"Do you think they've come to help us, Skipper?" Bowen asked.

Jane gasped, her eyes locked on the darkness moving toward them and holding tight onto *Altares*. "No," she said. "They're not here to help us."

The vessel stalked closer, its enormity bathing the light ship in its shadow. From the darkness, a blinding electric-blue spark flashed out. *Altares* quaked.

"They're firing on us," Anna said.

Masters confirmed the claim. "They just took out the forward laser!"

The radio chirped.

The chill engulfing Jane worsened. She shook her head. "Don't answer them, Dad. *Please.*"

But the signal couldn't be wished away, and the massive vessel was now near enough to be seen without the ship's cameras. It loomed directly ahead of them, its geometry difficult to classify. The spaceship's ebon skin lacked the recognizable symmetry of all known craft. It bulged at one end, tapered at the other, was somewhat oval in its center though not precise. The superstructure's surface bore no running lights or engine ports. Still, there was something familiar about the design to Jane. While she struggled to make the connection, Masters activated the link between vessels.

"This is Harry Masters, captain of the Earth Space Authority light ship *Altares*. Please identify yourself. Over."

Dead air poured out of the receiver.

"I repeat," Masters started. "This is —"

The receiver crackled with static, then the old woman's voice answered. "*Jane.*"

Jane tensed. The air around her grew too heavy to breathe. Her heart beat a tattoo against her ribcage. The boundaries of *Altares*' Flight Deck dissolved in a sea of black dots.

"*Jane, do you hear me?*"

The voice was no longer coming over the

radio but speaking directly to her. Jane reached down, intending to grip the armrests, but the copilot's chair was gone. She found herself standing in darkness, the air cool and bitter with a fetor of char. This was no dream experienced as a result of passing out due to the Photon Drive's acceleration to fantastic speeds, no. It was a nightmare being experienced in real time.

"I'm here, Jane," the old woman continued. "Right here. Long last, we have come together."

Jane spun around.

The darkness slithered.

"Where am I?" Jane asked.

"Don't you know?"

A sense of clarity washed over her, despite Jane's paralyzing terror. Her mind connected the dots, and she remembered why the alien ship's configuration seemed so familiar.

It was how *Altares* had looked on the screen, the live feed projected from Space Station Delta's long-range cameras, all crunched up and caving in upon herself.

"Why, Jane, this is your home. The light ship *Altares*."

Chapter Sixteen

Home, on Rankine Lane.

There were flowers in bloom, and a sultry summer breeze that stirred the fragrance of the cottage garden and fresh-cut grass. She was younger, not yet forced to grow up because of one parent's death and the other's need to escape, to get as far away as was humanly possible. So far, in fact, as to lead to the very heart of the Milky Way Galaxy. That version of Jane knew she was loved and happy. But love and happiness were illusions, just as the flowers were, and Jane saw through them.

Static crackled beside Jane's ears. She came out of her fugue and found herself surrounded by shadows.

"You're lying," Jane said. "This isn't home."

The old woman dismissed her claim with

a humorless laugh. "Don't you recognize the light ship *Altares*?"

"We're not on the *Altares*!"

"Not the *Altares* you know, but the one that comes soon after. The one you created when the ship surpassed the speed of light. This is an *Altares* trapped between the present and future, coming ever closer to being the only true reality. Through me, you are witness to the future that you and your crew have created. A paradox in time, if you like."

"A temporal paradox?" Jane said.

"A causality loop, to be precise," the old woman growled. "One event born of another. We are here because of what you and the others did!"

Jane sucked down a deep breath. The bitter scorched-metal odor in the air burned inside her lungs. "We haven't done anything wrong. We're explorers."

"Oh? Well, dear young explorer, contemplate the results of your mission to the stars."

Lights lit before her, blinding against the palette of darkness. The lights expanded and took shapes. The largest formed a globe of the Earth, only the vision projected was that of the dead world she'd glimpsed in her earlier nightmares. The oceans had boiled away, leaving desolation, desert. High in orbit around the lifeless planet was the vast space station in the shape of a double helix. Seeing it filled Jane with fresh dread.

"That's where they all go, after we return to the Earth," the woman said. "Humanity's last stand...only so few of the survivors are even remotely human after their exposure to what comes home on *Altares*. They'd spent so many years looking to the stars for answers instead of focused upon fixing what they'd broken."

"I don't understand."

"Don't you, Jane?" the woman asked, again her words more taunt than actual question. "Then let me help you to see the rest."

A shadow stirred, mostly out of view behind the vibrant hologram of the dead world. Footsteps clacked across the floor, their cadence heavy and uneven, accompanied by labored breaths.

"We, too fell into the black hole's hunger," the owner of that voice whispered. "And we managed to pull free thanks to the energy of the superluminal particle still trapped inside the Photon Drive. Only exceeding the speed of light while held by the black hole's gravity and the intense crushing forces changed us."

The shadow drifted closer. Jane backed away, matching the woman's advance through retreat. She already sensed the misshapen outline edging into view might drive her mad. She shuffled backward, over the uneven incline of the deck. No, this wasn't *Altares*—it couldn't be!

Then she crunched over something. By the vague light cast by the hologram, Jane saw it was the content of the fourth satellite launched into orbit at Alpha Centauri. The scroll, discarded from its protective cylinder.

"Jane," the shadow sang.

It rushed toward her, its multitude of limbs skittering across the distance. More than two hands seized hold of her, drawing the girl back. In the light of the dead future of Planet Earth, the full horror of what she faced registered. The old woman was only *partly* woman. The rest of her anatomy was comprised of mech and cables, connecting her to the scorched ship's innards like an umbilical cord, or intestines.

Worse than that was the glimpse of the old woman's face. Despite the years and technology forced upon it, Jane recognized that, too.

Because it was her face.

"Look, Jane," her future self commanded. "Look upon all that you have wrought!"

She fell into the hypnotic pull of the woman's eyes, which lit like monitors. And there, she saw—

—saw *Altares* collapsing in upon herself as the light ship attained the speed to break free from the black hole's grasp. Bowen, Anna, David, and her father...they hadn't survived the escape intact. Dead. No...*absorbed* into the buckling metal and conduit, becoming one with

Altares. The light ship, alive after a fashion, transformed by the forces that had turned space and time inside out. Her father, merged with the ship's mech. An eternity of suffering for them all.

She saw herself, the sole survivor. Only she'd no more survived than the Bowen family or Harry Masters. The long voyage back to Earth—there'd been nowhere else to go. The resulting chaos. The conflagration. The end game, in orbit. That gargantuan space station was now a hollow shell, scene of untold crimes and filled with the ghosts of a dead race.

"I'm the last human being," Future-Jane said in her thoughts. "The last living member of our people."

The paradox had crossed that alternative future time line with their present, Jane understood, her mind racing. At Alpha Centauri, the scroll—they'd all set their hands upon the cylinder before launching the commemorative time capsule into orbit around the red dwarf star. Only it hadn't contained enough harvestable DNA for the purposes of the abomination holding her prisoner.

"To undo what's been done to me," Future-Jane said aloud, rousing Jane from the nightmare spell of her thoughts. "To return me to fully human form. So to accomplish that, I need *you*."

The abomination raised one of her limbs. Sharp metallic points jutted out from the burned tips of fingers.

Jane attempted to turn away and shake free. This wasn't possible, no — she was still aboard *Altares*, strapped to the copilot's seat! Her father was alive. So were the Bowens.

Wake up, Jane, her mind attempted.

Cold, sharp metal worked through her long hair and brushed the tender skin at the nape of her neck. More metal pressed against her palm. Jane realized she'd dipped her hand inside her jacket pocket, seeking comfort from the talisman. She pulled out Winnie's snowflake dog tag and brandished it like a weapon.

The horror released her and drew away.

"What?" Future-Jane gasped. The old woman's cruel eyes softened. "*Winter?*"

"We can't return to Earth," Jane said. "We can't go home to Rankine Lane."

The darkness around her shattered, driven out by the brightness and clean landscape of *Altares'* Flight Deck.

"Jane," Masters repeated, shaking her. "Jane, do you hear me?"

Jane woke from the psychic connection with her future self. Her dark glimpse into that horrific tomorrow was ended, but not the danger it posed.

"It's still closing on us, Skipper," Bowen said. "Alien contact is moving in to dock with *Altares!*"

Jane looked. Beyond the space window, the dark *Altares* surged closer, its scorched hull nearly filling the glass from end to end.

"Dad," Jane said, "we can't let that ship come here. And we can't go home. Not ever."

Masters eyes studied her without blinking. "Then what can we do?"

Anna chimed in. "Harry, my instruments are acting haywire, but keep your fingers crossed. I think that black hole is rotating."

"What does that mean?" Jane asked.

"It may mean we have a chance. Some say that if you go *through* a rotating black hole, you end up in another universe—or even a new dimension. We don't know. But if we do survive it, there's no way back."

"And if it's non-rotating?" David posed.

"Then we'll be crushed out of existence."

"Skipper," Bowen prompted.

He tipped a look up to the screen. The dark *Altares* was on final approach to intercept them.

"Causal loop," Jane said. "Dad, if they come aboard, it's too late. The loop is completed, and all is lost—for us as well as the Earth!"

Masters exhaled. "That's it. There's nothing more we can do. To escape now, we'd have to travel faster than light. Now, you've heard what Anna said—nobody knows what it's like to travel through a black hole. But we've all gotten a glimpse at what happens with *that*."

He tipped his chin toward the screen.

"So let's not panic, just help each other all we can and hope we make it."

Dark *Altares* held on.

'Are you ready, Jane?"

Jane nodded.

"Anna?" Masters called.

She was.

The other, larger ship finalized its approach. On Masters' order, Jane kicked in the port steering rockets. *Altares* banked to starboard. Aided along by the black hole's insatiable gravity drag, *Altares* completed her turn and now faced the giant's maw. This also put their back to the other ship.

"Do it, Anna," Masters ordered. "Open fire!"

Anna thumbed the laser controls. *Altares*' aft cannon lashed out. Turned up to full strength, the powerful electric-blue beam slammed into the section of charred hull from which the magnetic beam holding onto them emitted. A spectacular explosion mushroomed up from the hostile spaceship's superstructure. *Altares* pulled free.

"Now hold on!" Masters called out to the crew.

He punched up their speed. *Altares* shot toward the singularity.

Protests shouted over the radio but were soon replaced by static. The dark *Altares* gave chase. For several more seconds, it registered on the screen. Then it winked out and was gone from view.

"We're entering the black hole," Bowen said.

Chapter Seventeen

She had been constructed in orbit, mostly in the massive hangars of Space Station Delta also serving the new Epsilon project. A shining example of the Space Authority's commitment to learning all they could about the universe and applying that enlightenment to improving conditions on the mother planet, *Altares* took more than two years to complete, another four months to test, and six more on top of that to train her crew of five.

The light ship's skeletal frame was still being assembled when the Authority named her—her identity chosen from the potential titles on a list submitted by school children, the winning entry from the country of Portugal.

"Why *Altares*?" Jane had asked her father.

They were in the open-air atrium at Spaceport Alpha, at the start of their training.

Harry Masters tipped a glance up to the sky—blue, but with clouds drifting in from the west. Another passenger shuttle was on its way up to Delta Station containing personnel involved with the construction work on either Space Station Epsilon or the light ship that would soon become their home.

"It means 'altars'—like the kind used in the Mexican Day of the Dead ceremonies."

"Altars? For worship?"

Masters shook his head. "No, the meaning is different. *Altares* are made out of respect for those who've died and left us, but aren't to be forgotten. Done in their honor."

The shuttle sailing over their heads accelerated, creating a thunderous boom that carried over the base and echoed across the horizon.

"Our *Altares* is a tribute to Newton, Galileo, Einstein…and to your mother, Jane."

Jane remembered their conversation as the light ship *Altares* plunged into the dark, swirling vortex of the black hole.

Masters reached toward the Photon Drive controls. What should have taken a fraction of a second drew out with the weight of a minute. Time had fallen off its tracks. He attempted to cut the engines—gravitational drag was doing the rest. The Flight Deck was plunged into shadows.

Anna lifted both hands to her temples.

The agony was excruciating. In addition to its hunger for the light ship, the singularity feasted on her cries of pain.

Outside the ship, streamers of light swallowed up by the black hole chased *Altares* in, forming a kaleidoscope of bright color around her hull.

Bowen grabbed at Anna, but she had fallen away to a distance that seemed miles not inches from his fingers. David was down, too. The waves of agony pulsing through *Altares* knocked the navigator aside. As he fell, the stress flipped Masters out of the pilot's chair. Jane extended her arms to ward off the pain. But the misery continued.

The dark *Altares*—Jane wondered if this was that crucial moment in that horrifying alternate timeline, when the ship's engines had found the muster to go faster than light and rocket them out of the black hole. That version of *Altares* had been crushed, singed, her crew altered irrevocably. The very walls of the ship seemed to be closing in on them now, the pain becoming unbearable.

The others had been absorbed by those walls. Absorbed into the fabric of *Altares*.

Jane looked up. Masters stood beside the wall of computers, his hand outstretched toward her. Behind him, the light ship warped like the surface of a pond overcome by ripples after a stone has been skipped over the water. Jane reached for him. The tips of their fingers brushed. The pulsations worsened, driving Masters closer to the ship's mechanism, and Jane away. The Navigation Area blurred around her, then Monitoring, the Crew's Quarters. *Altares* was collapsing in upon herself, crunching together.

The force about to destroy them knocked Jane all the way into the Photon Drive compartment.

Somehow, Anna reached David. She wrapped her arms around the boy, a mother's protection nothing when compared to the power seeking to claim their lives.

The kaleidoscopic effect surrounding the light ship invaded through the space windows and portholes in dazzling flashes of gold, red, and violet.

Altares was coming apart, fracturing. Worse, *reflecting* in that light as the fantastic stresses inside the black hole turned time and space inside out.

Jane sensed it, that replication of *Altares*. Facing the nearest porthole, she saw a second version of the light ship form beside the original. Two *Altares*. Two Janes. The unthinkable future they'd sought to avoid by opting to enter the black hole could not be escaped.

Two Annas. Two Davids.

The paradox that had led to the creation of the dark *Altares* and, ultimately, the destruction of the Earth was unfolding around her. Soon, the Photon Drive would kick in, powered past the speed of light by superluminal tachyon energies.

Two Harry Masters. Two Tom Bowens.

Anna's grip on David faltered. Jane saw one pass through the other. The reality of flesh and mech blurred.

Two realities, sharing one space…

Two *Altares*, racing in tandem through the searing effulgence of light.

The sound, the light, grew unbearable. At any moment, Jane expected *Altares* to catch fire and implode in upon herself. The future she'd glimpsed could not be avoided.

"*Jane,*" a woman's voice called.

It wasn't the horror from that other light ship, the Future-Jane of nightmares and endings. No. Familiar, she tracked it to the section of deck directly in front of the Photon Drive. Impossible!

"Hold on Jane," her mother said.

Winnie sat obediently beside Sylvia Masters, the dog's tail wagging. There were others, too — people she didn't know, but somehow recognized. Hundreds. *Thousands*, filling the rear compartment, bathed in light. All the brilliant thinkers and souls throughout history that had gotten them to this instant in time.

A breathtaking view spread outside *Altares*' portholes in the form of vast bands of violet-colored gas plumes lit by silver stars. Nearer by, a blue globe appeared off their prow. The light ship flew on toward the planet.

Anna moved from the porthole to the center of the Flight Deck, the stunned look on her face mirrored by the rest of the crew.

"Where are we?" she asked.

Masters stared out the space window at the blue planet, growing larger in front of them with each second. "I don't know. A different part of the universe."

Bowen approached. "No, it's a *new* universe."

"It's a new world," David said, a smile lighting his face.

Jane gazed out the porthole beside him. "It looks like we'll get to visit an alien planet after all, David."

Energy and exuberance surged through Jane. But the emotion darkened as soon as it released. New world? What about the old—the Earth? She set her hand against the length of corrugated metal wall at the base of the porthole, only to recoil. A dark *Altares*? A horrific end to their journey, with dire consequences for the Earth?

But even as Jane attempted to remember the details, they were dissolving from her memory, like the fragments of a dream. The malaise faded completely, and she allowed herself to bask in the joy of a new beginning none of them had thought possible.

Altares assumed a high orbit around the blue planet. Readings poured in, along with damage reports.

"Our forward laser cannon suffered serious damage," Anna said. "It's going to take extra-vehicular activity to repair."

Masters continued his evaluation on the Flight Deck's systems. "We'll schedule an EVA before making planet-fall," he said.

Given their circumstances, the *Altares* had fared well. What was broken could be fixed, and the crew's spirits had lifted. He cast a glance at Jane, working the light ship in her orbit around the alien world, and smiled. Behind them, the Bowens were engaged in carrying out this exciting new stage of the *Altares* Mission.

We knew it was impossible to return to Earth and to our own space and time, Masters thought. *We must come to terms with an existence here on the other side of the black hole.*

Jane adjusted their heading. "Maintaining course," she said. "*Altares* in orbit."

The blue globe spun beneath them, its surface lit by the warm glow of its sun. *Altares* neared the terminator; soon, they'd enter the night side of the planet's face.

One thing is for sure, he agreed. *This is not the final word. Not the end but the beginning. A new universe? A new hope? Only time will tell.*

Altares turned the curve of the blue planet and flew into shadow.

Ahead, tomorrow waited.

Afterword

I grew up in a small, enchanted cottage nestled between a lake and big woods, and was raised on a healthy diet of classic TV Science Fiction and creature double features. I have vague memories of Gerry Anderson's Supermarionation shows from an early age — they ran on Saturdays in my boyhood years. But then, when I was five, *U.F.O.* premiered and I was smitten as well as haunted by the premise. Five years later on an early September Tuesday night, I sat cross-legged on our living room floor, anxiously awaiting the start of *Space: 1999,* and can honestly say that experience changed my life. The very next day, I picked up my pen and began to write what would amount to my very first fan fiction story. Since then, I've penned hundreds of *1999* short stories, novellas, and novels, all for the endless love I have for that universe and characters — and those original tales written when I was a boy are still archived to this day in my writing room's filing cabinets more than four decades later. That brilliant outer space parable made me a writer. In my career, I've written for film, TV—two episodes of Paramount's *Star Trek: Voyager* series, had novels published (two via Home Shopping Network for their 'Escape With Romance' line), won awards (including an Honorable Mention in the Roswell Award in short SF writing), and worked for national magazines, including the former Sci Fi Channel's namesake publication, during which I interviewed Martin Landau, *1999*'s heroic Commander Koenig, when he starred in 1998's *The X-Files* movie. But my passion for writing owes to that night when the courageous men and women of Moonbase Alpha invited me along on their journey through the cosmos.

Not long after that beginning point, I found myself seated on the same patch of living room floor in front of the boxy, ugly TV set hooked to rabbit ears for Mister Anderson's made-for-TV movie pilot, *The Day After Tomorrow: Into Infinity*. Not only were most of the principle actors also associated with *Space: 1999*, but the script was penned by Johnny Byrne, who had written some of the most memorable of my beloved obsession's episodes. Again, I felt welcomed along for the adventure. Flash forward to a late September weekend in 2016. I was with members of my writers' group at a retreat house set beside a roaring waterfall.

The message came in—would I be interested in adapting Mr. Byrne's pilot script into a novelization to be published by Anderson Productions? My first thought was that if the me that is now could go back in time and tell the me that was then about this latest project, he'd be completely overjoyed. Or faint dead away from the shock. My next was an ominous sense of dread that I wouldn't be able to honor Gerry Anderson and Johnny Byrne's vision. I'd met Mr. Byrne twice at the *Space: 1999* conventions held in 1999 and 2000, and have great respect for the man and his work. I also felt supremely honored to have been asked.

     One of my last responsibilities at the end of 2016 was to print up a physical copy of the script, which I'd already read twice before, to aid in my tackling the adaptation. I three-hole-punched it, brass bradded the top and bottom holes, and had it on my desk front and center for three months. I think now, as I did then, that Mr. Byrne's work is genius. The sense of love he had for this particular project is clear, and almost radiates off the page. A writer's original script is always dissected, dialogue streamlined on set for flow, and scenes get moved around, but it's such a delight to see the original framework before that happens—the writer's vision in its purest distillation. From early on, I wanted to keep Johnny Byrne's dialogue intact. I was able to utilize most of the original material that got cut in the adaptation, and that material made it possible for me to craft my additions to the story of the *Altares* mission.

I had the original TV pilot playing in the background, pausing it scene-by-scene, matched up to the open script while I wrote. There were nights when the *Into Infinity* theme serenaded my dreams. I write all my first drafts longhand, on lined paper. So my notepad was catty-cornered over the open script, with my laptop at an angle close enough nearby so that I could stop and backtrack or scroll forward.

I loved the five principles of *Into Infinity*, and I'd like to think I connected with all of them. But in particular, I grew close with Jane Masters, who is the primary narrator of the adaptation, and Anna Bowen. Anna carries a devastating secret aboard with her, whereas Jane becomes involved in the growing mystery that sets the tone for the story's climax. Of course, it was easy for me to love the TV pilot's adult cast. Nick Tate — pilot Harry Masters — was Alan Carter in *Space: 1999*. Brian Blessed (Tom Bowen) played Doctor Cabot Rowland in the first season, and Maya's father Mentor in Year Two. The lovely Joanna Dunham was Raan's daughter in the episode "Missing Link". Even Don Fellows, who played Controller Forbes, had a minor role in *Space: 1999* — as the newscaster seen in the pilot episode, "Breakaway". Actress Katharine Levy's range as Jane Masters was both sublime and powerful, which made writing about her character a true joy.

For the adaptation, I was tasked with expanding upon the original storyline by coming up with certain new elements. I set out writing and, by the second chapter, came to a realization regarding two of the main characters, Anna and Tom Bowen and their marriage. As soon as this thought manifested, my pen began to fly across the page and worked the new wrinkle in to what Mr. Byrne had already established. Then late one winter night while a snowstorm raged outside our home, I woke up in the dark from a dream involving the *Altares* mission that left me scrambling for paper and pen—luckily, I keep both handy in a drawer at bedside. After jotting down my notes about the dark *Altares* and the vision of Earth that Jane glimpses in her nightmares, I snuggled under the covers and rehashed what the dream had been about. I couldn't get down to my home office quick enough the following morning to work the new storyline into the adaptation.

Have I succeeded in this project? That decision, of course, belongs to you, the Reader. Is there a future for the crew aboard *Altares*? I sure hope so, and welcome the opportunity to return with the Masters and Bowen families on their adventures far beyond known space. One thing is for certain: their story is still relevant, and still being discussed more than four decades after the original movie broadcast.

--Gregory L. Norris, July 2017

Printed in Great Britain
by Amazon